THE PERPETUAL PENITENT

AN ADAM FRALEY MYSTERY

HENRY HOFFMAN

THE PERPETUAL PENITENT
Copyright © 2019 by Henry Hoffman

ISBN: 978-1-68046-808-3

Melange Books, LLC
White Bear Lake, MN 55110
www.melange-books.com

Published in the United States of America.

Cover Design by Ashley Redbird Designs

"The man hath penance done, and penance more will do."

—Samuel Taylor Coleridge
The Rime of the Ancient Mariner

———

"I think you're surrendering to dejection. You must shake yourself up, look at life straight on. I know it's hard, but…"

—Leo Tolstoy
Anna Karenina

CHAPTER ONE

October 1996

"My name is Carolina Coulter, Mr. Fraley. Many of my friends call me Cara for short."

At the mention of the name, Adam's office manager across the room at once shifted her eyes from her computer screen to the young woman sitting in front of her boss's desk.

"I discovered early on four-syllable first names invite alternatives," his visitor added.

"I like Carolina, and please call me Adam."

The tallish young woman had a dignified manner about her. A lemon-yellow blouse and dark blue dress fit favorably over her slender figure. Her sandy blonde hair was curled to the shoulders, framing an expressive face highlighted by crystal blue eyes.

"Now, what I can I do for you?" he asked.

She shifted in her chair, crossed her legs, and smoothed her dress before responding in a soft voice. "Perhaps I should start from the very beginning."

"The beginning is always a good place to start. I have found in many cases it often mitigates the confusion that follows," he said, taking a pencil in hand.

She nodded, as if prepared to shed her reluctance. "Five years ago, I could unequivocally state my family was leading a charmed life with hardly a worry in the world. My father had embarked on a successful career in high finance, following a short but successful career in professional football. Perhaps you've heard of him. His name is David Coulter."

"Yes," Adam said, and with it, an inkling of where this was headed came to mind.

"I was sixteen at the time and in high school. My sole sibling was a three-year-old sister. Her name was Sadie. She was the treasure of the family. Due to the age difference between us, there of course was no sibling rivalry to speak of. While our father was pursuing his business career, our stay-at-home mom devoted all of her time and energy to taking care of us on the home front, seeing to it that our formative years were rewarding ones. Those were very happy days, but the happiness all came crashing down nearly five years ago in one terrible moment." She paused to catch a breath. "You may already be aware of what I'm about to say to you since it made the papers at the time."

Adam nodded, acknowledging his general awareness. It made the papers all right, he recalled, though even hard-bitten editors must have thought twice of the question of whether to include it. The compromise was to bury it on the inside pages. "But please go on," he quickly added, wanting to hear it directly and in detail from her.

She took a deep breath before continuing. "Well, one day my father was rushing to meet some friends of his for their usual Saturday morning golf outing. He was running late due to a last-minute business call he had to make. Once he finished it, he rushed out the front door, jumped into the family SUV and began to back out of the drive, unaware that Sadie, blocked from his view by the car, was playing in the driveway. My mother was in the front yard tending to some flower beds and was also unaware of the danger. In his haste my father backed the vehicle over Sadie..." She halted her story as words became difficult and tears began to well in her eyes. "Sorry…"

"That's okay. Take your time," Adam said, at which point his office manager rose from her chair and deftly strode across the floor.

"Excuse me, can I interrupt you for a moment?" she asked in a low voice.

"Sure," he said, then turned to his potential client. "Carolina, this is my office manager, Tamra Fugit."

The two women acknowledged each other's presence with polite nods. "I have a few errands to run, if that's okay," Tamra said.

"Fine," Adam replied, fully aware the real reason she was exiting the room was to give them a measure of privacy, something their cramped one-room office did not allow.

Having regained her composure, Carolina continued with her account of the incident. "Anyway, the first thing I heard was my mother screaming outside. Seconds later my father burst open the front door and rushed to the telephone to call 9-1-1. I will never forget the look on his face, as he breathlessly explained to the dispatcher the reason for his call. The emergency crew arrived quickly but it was all in vain. She was killed instantly and by a father who adored her. The image of her lifeless little body with my father and mother bending over her in anguish is one that will forever haunt me as it has them."

She hunched her shoulders ever so slightly, "Well, that's the story in a nutshell and now you're probably wondering why I'm here."

"Yes…what is it I can do for you?" he asked, his curiosity stirred.

"I'm here to ask you to fix a family," she said straightforwardly.

"In what way?" he asked, taken aback by the directness and breadth of the request.

"In the beginning there was forgiveness all around, from me, my mother, and close friends of the family, all directed in good faith at my father. Nevertheless, a tension simmered below the surface in the aftermath, particularly between my mother and father. Ironically, what aggravated matters was my father's prior insistence on family safety. For instance, my mother and I had long lobbied for a backyard swimming pool, but he was adamantly against it. 'How many times do you hear on the news of a toddler drowning in the family pool?' he would ask with Sadie in mind. Then there were the innocent comments to follow that unintentionally brought the incident back into focus…"

Carolina suddenly suspended her line of thought, as though wary of feeding a demon that had occupied her mind far too long.

"Comments like…?" Adam asked in a quiet tone, nudging her along ever so easily while at the same time probing for as much background information as he could without appearing overly intrusive.

She exhaled another deep breath. "Like the time not long after the incident the three of us got in the car to head out somewhere and the first thing my mother said to him was 'Careful' as he began to back the car down the drive. Her simple word of caution was like sticking a dagger in him."

"And the end result of the friction?"

"The end result was the end of the marriage—not formally, but in reality. My father and mother loved each other deeply but could not cope with the fallout despite months of counseling. Things had spiraled down to the point where the unsaid between them spoke louder than what was said."

"What was your living status at the time?" Adam asked.

"By then I had graduated from high school and went away to college to pursue a liberal arts degree. I carried a full load year round and managed to complete the required course work in three years. Following graduation, I took a job with a public relations firm here in town and moved out of the house. To make a long story short, one day while I was still in school, my mother called to let me know my father had quit his job, packed up his belongings, and left the house without so much as a hint as to why or where. The why part we could pretty much guess, the where part we had no idea. That is why I have come to you for help."

"You reported his disappearance to the police?"

"Yes, but they quickly pointed out to us he was an adult, not a minor, and could do whatever he wanted, as long as he did not break the law. Furthermore, unless there was evidence, he was a victim of foul play or was in imminent danger, they had no reason to pursue the matter."

"How long ago was this?"

"A little over five years."

"Why did you wait until now to seek out private assistance?"

"We had convinced ourselves he was just taking time off to clear his head and that eventually he would return home. But time got away from us and he never did. By then, my mother had come to accept the notion he would never return."

"But you didn't."

"I agreed there was a good chance he would not return but I was not ready to accept it without some kind of confirmation."

"There's been no word from him at all?"

"None."

"Is your mother presently living alone?"

"Yes, and that brings up another matter. My mother is now fully convinced he's not coming back and, as I said, she may be right. It is now officially five years since he went missing. In Florida you can petition to have someone declared legally dead if they are missing for a continuous period of five years and if their absence is not satisfactorily explained after a diligent search and inquiry. She already has hired a lawyer to help her with the petitioning."

"And the diligent search and inquiry is where I come in," he said.

"Yes, and there's one more issue at play. There is a new man in my mother's life. They plan on getting married once the petition is approved."

"Do you approve?"

"Of her getting married or him?"

"Both."

"If it is certain my father is not coming back and is declared legally dead, I have no objection, though I'm not sure it is out of love she is entering into this marriage. She is terribly lonely and is desperate for permanent companionship. As for her beau, I've only met him a few times. He seems okay, but I feel confident in stating he in no way measures up to my father in his feelings toward my mother."

"What's his background?"

"He's a medical doctor. That's about all I know."

"Does your mother know you have sought out a private investigator?"

"No. At this point I'm not sure whether she would approve. Like I said, she seems to have accepted the idea he is not coming back."

"Do you know if your mother's lawyer has any intention of conducting a formal search for your father?"

"No, though I should correct what I said about her hiring a lawyer. It was her beau who did the hiring—at least that's what she said."

"Do you know the name of the lawyer?"

"No."

"So, if I take the case, there may be two entities in search of your father."

"Yes, but I have no confidence in the other entity. They could well be searching for someone they don't want to find. That should tell you how much effort is going into their search. If there is a hunt for him, I'm almost positive it is a *pro forma* one."

"Gotcha," he said.

Adam set aside the pencil he was taking notes with, nudged his chair back a bit from the desk, stretched his legs out, and clasped his hands in his lap. "Well, Carolina, here's what we're facing. We do not have the resources law enforcement officials have in tracking down missing individuals. They have ties to vast worldwide information networks, not to mention subpoena powers to access private records. We, on the other hand, fly by the seat of our pants, or should I say trudge along on the soles of our shoes, relying heavily on input from our clients. So, let me ask you this as a starting point: Do you have any idea where your father may have taken off to?"

She gave a slight shrug. "If I did, I would have already checked it out long ago."

"Fair enough," Adam said, dispensing with the obvious. "Then let me rephrase the question. Was there any one place your father particularly enjoyed visiting—say, while on vacation or on some sort of assignment—that he let it be known was a favorite refuge from any stress he might be under?"

"Our vacations were standard fare—visits to the national parks, Disney World, the beaches. He always thought cross-country train travel was relaxing and often talked about getting one of those long-term Amtrak passes that allowed you to travel anywhere on their route at any time. He said he would like to sit in the club car and watch the world go by."

"Anything else?"

She thought a moment. "Our family was active in the church…"

"Sorry to interrupt—which church?" he asked.

"Queen of Peace. Do you know of it?"

"Yes. What sort of family activity?"

"My parents oftentimes attended out-of-town retreats sponsored by the church. My father especially liked the downtime."

"Where out of town?"

"Calvary Monastery, north of Orlando."

"What else?" Adam asked.

She wrinkled her brow in thought. "Well, I don't know whether you would call this getting away from it all, but my parents also volunteered for a couple of church-sponsored missions to Haiti to help with recovery efforts following several major storms that ended up devastating the country. They both had a strong altruistic streak in them."

"Were those their only overseas adventures?"

"Yes. My mother had a fear of flying which limited their long-distance traveling."

"Anything else?"

She again shrugged before continuing. "Well, my father did have a dentist friend who moved his practice and family to Whitefish, Montana, a number of years ago. The reason I mention it is that he often talked about taking a cross-country train trip up there to visit him."

"What's his name?"

"Dan Conner, if I recall correctly."

Adam continued his scribbling.

"You're going to accept the assignment?" she asked, taking note of his notes.

"Yes, I am, Carolina, but I want to advise you it could be costly. This case is about as far away from a slam dunk as you can get. He could be anywhere in the world or dead and buried for all we know. The fact no one has reported seeing him is a discouraging sign in itself. He was a person very much in the limelight, after all."

"I can pay you. Money is no problem. My father made sure long before he disappeared that me and my mother were taken care of financially."

Adam unclasped his hands and straightened his lean frame in his chair. "Okay, here is what I need before you leave. Do you have a photo of your father on you, preferably the most current one available? Also, I will need a current one of you."

"I don't have them on me, but I do have several of each at home. I can fetch them and have them back in your office this afternoon," she said. "Do you need one of my mother? I'm not certain if I have a recent one of her. She's always had a strong aversion to cameras."

"No, those of you and your father will do. You also will need to leave your contact information with my office manager. You can do that when you return with the photos."

Adam rose to bid her goodbye, at once second-guessing his decision to take on the case. When it came to family dysfunctions, emotions run high. Already, he was as apprehensive as a rookie cop responding to a domestic disturbance call.

———

"The moment I heard her mention his name, a bell rang," Tamra said, rehashing the original incident and Adam's detailed account of the interview following her return to the office. "What a terrible burden to bear. I remember thinking at the time there was no way the family was going to survive that kind of personal trauma."

"It appears they may not," Adam said from across the room. "Some choose their cross to bear, mitigating the burden. Others, like the Coulter family, have it handed to them. Unfortunately, it's often an unbearable one. When it comes to family tragedies, the death of a child is the worst of the worst. What makes it especially burdensome is the realization the father had a direct hand in his daughter's death. It's one thing for a parent or guardian to leave the backyard swimming pool gate open, allowing a toddler to wander into dangerous territory and accidentally drown. It's another to directly back over your child, crushing the life out of them. Definitely makes most everyone else's problems seem trivial in comparison."

"I suppose in a case like that you could be charged with reckless driving or negligence of some kind, could you not?"

"It would take a heartless prosecutor to bring that case, I would think."

"Agreed. So what made you take the case?"

"No way could I turn down a request—more like a plea—to ease the pain they're going through. As you've heard me say, putting a family back together is one of the most challenging and satisfying aspects of this job. Carolina made it sound like this was her last shot at making things whole again. Plus, there's another reason," he quickly added.

"Here comes the real reason," Tamra opined.

"Maybe...maybe not."

"Care to share?"

"Sure," he said, sinking back in his chair and clasping his hands above his head. "When I was about eight or nine, I played Pee Wee football."

"You were a football player?" she interrupted.

"Is that beyond imagining?" he shot back. "If you must know, I never made it past the Pee Wee level."

Tamra tossed him a teasing smile, a strand of her auburn hair falling across one of her deep green eyes. "That I can believe," she said, brushing away the hair.

"May I go on?"

"Please do," she said.

"Back then, my father decided he would sign me up for a one-day youth football camp here in Tampa as a birthday present. It was organized and run by a couple of pro football players. On the day of the camp my father was unexpectedly called to work. One of the guys he worked with had phoned in sick. My father was assigned to replace him, so my mother ended up taking me to the camp. I spent the day doing wind sprints, jumping jacks, push-ups, hopscotching through a track of tires, pushing against a blocking sled, and learning how to pass, throw, and catch a football. All of the basics were on display.

"It so happened one of the pro football players helping to run the camp was David Coulter. I recall him as being very patient in teaching us the fundamentals of the game. He wasn't just putting in his time there. He was making sure we were getting our money's worth. At the same time, my mother, who could care less about football, was up in the stands also displaying extra patience, off and on reading a book or monitoring me. It was nearly dusk by the time the camp ended. Anyway, as we were driving home, our car, a small sedan, had a blowout. The car skidded off the road, with the blown-out tire and wheel ending up in a deep rut. My mother tried to free it by gunning the motor and alternately shoving the clutch into drive and reverse to rock it back a forth, but it didn't work. We then tried to push it out but again failed. The truth was even if we got it back on level ground, we still had to change the tire, something neither of us had ever done. To make matters worse, there was no phone nearby to call for help. I could see my mother was becoming distraught. The road we had taken was a shortcut to the interstate and not a well-traveled one. A few cars passed by though none stopped to offer help. About that time, I offered to hoof it to find a gas station or a store of any kind, but my mother would have none of it. 'Someone will stop to help,' she said unconvincingly.

"She turned out to be right, however. No sooner had she said it than a Jeep pulled up behind us and out hopped a man the size of an NFL tight end. In fact, it was an NFL tight end. It was David Coulter. 'Adam!' he called out, remembering me from the camp. 'Looks like you've got yourself in a little jam there, buddy.'

"I introduced him to my mother, who appeared to be resisting an overwhelming temptation to throw her arms around him.

"Let's see if you and I can push this thing back onto the road while your mother steers it,' he said.

"We pushed and pushed and no thanks to me got the car back up on level ground. I then continued my heavy lifting—holding the flashlight while he changed the tire. My mother tried like hell to pay him for his efforts, but he would have none of it. 'Someday, when I grow old and feeble,' he told her, 'I too may end up on the side of the road in a rut, and hopefully, some young man like your son will stop to lend a hand. That would be the best repayment,' he said. And off he went."

"So, he is a hero of yours," said his office manager.

"For that night he sure was."

"Why didn't you tell this story to Carolina?"

"Because in the end, no matter how it turns out, this story will be about him, not me."

"Given his present state of mind, a psychologist might be more in order at this stage. His brain needs fixing first."

"More appropriate than a private eye like me, you mean?"

"Well at least in an advisory capacity."

"I'm sure the family has seen plenty of those. Speaking of which, that therapist who we helped move into the office above us a while back, isn't he a licensed psychologist?"

"I believe so."

"He said if he could ever return the favor, let him know. I think I'll pay him a visit in the morning. Maybe he can offer some insight into David Coulter's state of mind. Meantime, why don't you start digging into whatever public records are available online and see if you can come up with a clue as to where he might have landed."

"If only we had access to banking records like the police, so we could map out a paper trail." she pointed out. "Missing persons have to spend money too, after all."

"That's just one of the resources they have that we don't have," he said.

A smile formed on his office manager's face. "While you're busy lamenting what you just signed up for, do you want me to cheer you up with a bit of happy news?"

"Please."

"Noelle wants us to go out on a double date with her and Bobby Taylor."

Adam furrowed his brow. "What? My thirteen-year-old daughter…"

"Soon to be fourteen," Tamra quickly interjected.

"Okay, my soon-to-be fourteen-year-old daughter wants to go out on a double date with you and me. Whatever or whoever gave her that idea?" Adam asked, peering into his office manager's eyes as though she were the instigator.

"It wasn't my idea," Tamra said, recognizing the accusatory look on her boss's face. "She is a pretty girl, Adam, and the boys are going to start showing up at your door with increasing frequency, as you well know. Isn't it better for her to be upfront about it rather than sneaking off with some kid behind your back? She just wants the four of us to go out for a pizza together. She's looking for your approval."

"I told her she could start dating when she hits sixteen."

"It's really not a date. I shouldn't have called it that," she said. "It's more like a casual outing among friends."

"If ever there was a tragedy in the making, this is it," Adam said. "I never trusted that Bobby Taylor."

"According to Noelle, you've never met him."

"All the more reason for not trusting him."

CHAPTER TWO

MADISON DAVIS, PSYCHOLOGIST, SAT WITH HIS FEET PROPPED UP on his desk, nonchalantly perusing pages of a professional journal, when Adam strode into his office through an opened doorway. At first glance he could not help but note that the casual look presented by the thirty-something man not only applied to his office decor but his attire as well. A blue floral Hawaiian shirt hung loosely over his denim pants which stretched to the sock-less feet and tan loafers he was wearing. Casual Friday was casual every day for this guy, Adam reckoned.

"Adam Fraley!" Davis called out, tossing aside the journal and dropping his feet from the desk. "Have a chair," he beckoned, running a hand through his sandy blond hair, random strands of which touched the collar of his shirt. A bronzed, narrow face, burnished as much by a cosmetics bottle as the sun, Adam figured, completed the relaxed look.

"You said if you could ever return the favor of our lending you a hand in your move, to please let you know," Adam said from across his desk. "Well, here I am, asking for a favor in return."

"What is it I can do for you?"

Adam related the Coulter family story in detail, concluding with Carolina Coulter's decision to hire him.

"You're of the belief I am able to assist you in some way with the case?" Davis asked in a whisky voice that belied the youthful air about him.

"My office doesn't have the resources the cops do in tracking down a missing person. We have to rely on intuition—guesswork, if you will—to locate him. Given his state of mind, I thought you might have some ideas as to where he might have landed, that is if he's still alive."

Davis straightened himself in his chair, exchanging the relaxed look for a more formal business posture. "Having just located to this area, I don't recall the specific incident. However, I've had several clients in the past who faced similar dire circumstances arising from a traumatic family tragedy. And yes, you're absolutely right in thinking the incident as you describe it ranks among the most horrific when it comes to generating mental trauma. Let me ask you…is he a person of faith?"

"The entire family is," Adam answered.

"Christian?"

"Catholic."

A grin creased the psychologist's face. "One and the same in my world."

"Your world is what?"

"Put simply, a complex mishmash of mind and behavior. Nonetheless, as an avowed agnostic, I can tell you this. Mr. Coulter's God may forgive him, but the core issue driving him is that he can't forgive himself. Nor likely will he ever, given the nature of the event."

"So, on the chance it is forgiveness he is looking for, where does he find it?"

"He first finds it within his family," Davis stated confidently.

"According to his daughter, the family already has granted their forgiveness."

"No doubt on a surface level, Adam. Keep in mind there's a time factor involved when you're coping with the mental consequences of severe trauma. Forgiveness doesn't come easy in those cases. It requires a healing period and a healing period for a brain can be a lengthy process."

"Absent forgiveness, he what? Lapses into a suicidal state?"

"Possibly, but that goes against the tenets of his religion. The clients

I mentioned before…all practicing churchgoers…who found themselves burdened under similar severe circumstances often felt their sole hope for redemption was to devote the remainder of their lives to performing some kind of severe penance. Otherwise, the flood of damning thoughts would drown them in despair. The bottom line is the penance keeps them afloat. It is tantamount to a lifeboat. I categorize these people as the perpetual penitents. In their minds it is the sole alternative to giving up on life and turning suicidal, which, like I said, is contradictory to their religious convictions. In my opinion, your Mr. Coulter, if he is still alive and kicking, is likely engaged in some kind of serious penance. Perhaps that's a clue for you as to where he might have landed. Agree?"

Adam shrugged. "Could be. I asked his daughter what some of his favorite getaway activities were, places he liked to escape to in order to clear his head or ease his stress."

"And where were those places?" Davis asked.

"One you could describe as a succession of places. Apparently, he had a strong fondness for cross-country train trips."

Davis at once wrinkled his brow and shook his head. "I don't see that as a penance unless you happen to be sitting next to a loud-mouth for over a half a continent."

"Well then, how about this one—a monastic retreat? His daughter said he and her mother would occasionally attend a retreat at a monastery north of Orlando."

"What is he going to do there for any length of time? Become a groundskeeper? A handyman? He's certainly not qualified to become a member of the order, though he probably wishes he could. Living his life out as a monk might seem enticing to him, given the circumstances."

"One other activity she mentioned," Adam continued. "Her parents made several trips to Haiti through the years as part of church missions to help with relief efforts following a couple of devastating storms."

Davis threw up his hands. "Voila! There you have it—hard core missionary work—the stuff of saints and penitents. Any impoverished nation would do, but Haiti would be in his comfort zone, considering his past experiences there. It may be a good distance from here, but he undoubtedly has a contact or two from his previous work there."

"If that's the case, it's a tough way to live out your life, as you say," Adam noted.

"That's the point. It's the kind of penance a man in his state would impose on himself, short of committing hara-kiri."

Adam propped his elbows on the desk, resting his chin on laced fingers in contemplation of his next question. "If he happened to be sitting right here, what would you say to him?" he asked.

"I would say to him it was an accident, not a sin you committed, though I doubt it would alleviate his anguish, simply because the words were coming from the mouth of a professional. His guilt is never ending, unless by chance he finds it in himself to accept forgiveness. I don't mean for this to sound trite, but as I stated earlier, his only hope is to find it through his family. How he comes to find it, I do not know. Perhaps an outsider can steer him in the right direction," Davis said through a sly smile, suggesting who that outsider might be.

Adam nodded. "I thank you for your input. I'll see if I can put it to good use," he said, doubt again creeping into his decision to take on the task. Finding Coulter and bringing him back were two very different challenges, he came to realize.

Davis leaned back in his chair and cupped his hands in his lap. "Before you rush off, can I pose a question to you on an entirely different matter?"

"Sure," Adam responded, his interest piqued as to where this was headed.

"Your office manager—Tamra—is she spoken for?"

Adam was a bit taken aback by the question, but why should he be? It was not like Tamra lacked attention from men. Quite the contrary. "Yes, she's spoken for."

Davis cast a lethargic smile his way. "Can't say that comes as a surprise. She's a very attractive woman and appears to have an engaging personality. I didn't notice a ring on her finger so assumed she was single. Lucky guy…you know him?"

"Yes, I know him."

"An okay guy?"

"Yeah, an okay guy is a good way to describe him."

"She'd settle for an 'okay' guy?"

"Surprising—isn't it—what women will settle for?"

"Hands off then?"

"'Spoken for, hands off.' Doesn't one imply the other?"

"Tell him to close the deal, or someone else might come along and steal her away. That biological clock ticks fast for a woman, as I'm sure you know."

Adam nodded in a quick, dismissive manner as though the topic was one he cared not to discuss further. "Well, I'd better get back to work," he said, rising from his chair. "Again, I thank you for your input. You've provided me some good insight."

"Keep me informed," Davis called to him on his way to the door. "Not an easy task you have there...mending a broken mind. That is, if you're able to first locate its owner."

"Mending a mind is not my job, Madison. Like you said, that ultimately is the task of the family. On your second point, however, you're right...locating its owner and convincing him to return is my job."

———

Adam stood aside his office manager, relating the thoughts of Davis regarding the Coulter case, while pointedly excluding the guy's probes concerning her private life. "I think the possibility of Haiti as a landing spot for Coulter makes sense considering his past," he said. "I see it as a good starting point."

"You're planning on a trip there?"

"Yes, and relative to that, do you recall Pierre Gantt, the guy who painted our office for us a year or so ago?"

"Sure...the fellow from Louisiana. What's he got to do with the case?"

"I remember him telling me he had spent time in Haiti doing some subcontract work for a construction company. The reason they sent him there had a lot to do with his ability to speak Creole. If you recall, he was born and raised in Louisiana. I'm thinking it might be worth contacting him to see if he'd be interested in picking up some extra money serving as my guide."

"You best make it clear to him it's not a tour you have in mind."

"For sure, though he struck me as the adventurous type. Perhaps he's hankering for a taste of it…in a land he is familiar with to boot."

"You want his phone number? I still have it on file."

"Yes, and there is another trip I need to squeeze in this weekend before I head off to Haiti."

"Where's that?" she asked, scribbling down Gantt's number and handing it to him.

"Colorado."

His little announcement was met with downcast eyes and silence.

Adam reached out and gently laid a hand on her shoulder. "It's not what you think it is."

"Does it matter what I think?" she asked smartly. Before he could answer, she followed with a second. "Are you taking Noelle?"

"No, I'm not, which poses another question. I hate to ask, but can…"

"She can stay with me, Adam," Tamra interjected.

"Now that she's reached teenager status, she should be okay home alone for a night maybe—for a weekend, not so much. What do you think?"

"You're forgetting the Haiti trip right after."

"Oh…yeah."

"That means she and I will be spending a week or so together…right?"

"Are you sure you…"

"I don't mind at all, but remember, she has her heart set on that dinner date with Bobby you and I are to attend."

"I know. She keeps reminding me of it. Once I get the Colorado and Haiti trips out of the way, it's definitely next on the list."

"By the way, I did take the liberty of contacting Calvary Monastery to check if Mr. Coulter had paid them a visit recently," said Tamra. "I ended up talking to the monk who was in charge of organizing their retreats. He knew of Mr. Coulter from his past trips up there. However, he said there had been no sign of him in recent years. I also was able to contact the dentist, Dan Conner, in Montana. The answer was the same. He said he had not heard from him in some time."

"It's good you touched base with both. Better to verify than surmise before we head out elsewhere, only to find out later it was a wasted trip."

"Meanwhile, do you want me to check the public records on Coulter?"

"I doubt if anything significant will show up, but again, it's best we cover all the bases we can before we go the gumshoe route. Also, see if you can come up with a list of Catholic-run missions and churches in Haiti," he added.

Adam locked onto her eyes and slowly removed his hand from her shoulder, lightly brushing her cheek with the back of it as he did, prompting from her a wan smile. "I'll give Pierre a call," he said, forgoing further explanation for his trip to Colorado.

CHAPTER THREE

OFF IN THE DISTANCE, THE SOARING SNOW-CAPPED PEAKS OF THE Rockies burned brightly beneath the glare of an early morning sun as Adam's flight glided effortlessly along the landing path into Colorado Spring's airport. Waiting to greet him minutes later was Carlita Perez, the woman who had changed his life forever a few years back.

There had been little change in her appearance from the moment they first met. She continued to carry her trim frame with grace, flash the same wide smile across her olive-skinned face, and knot her long dark hair into a ponytail that lay over her shoulder.

"I thought we'd take a quick trip this morning to where it all started," she said, escorting him to her cream-colored, late-model Jeep.

"You mean the scene of the crime," he said, prompting a nod and a smile from her. "Well, you have to admit, it did turn out to be much more than a crime," she responded. Minutes later she had the Jeep on the interstate, heading south toward the turnoff that would ultimately take them to their destination. "Are you currently working on a case?"

"I'm always working on a case," he said, and proceeded to relate the details of the Coulter matter. "It's one I may regret taking on."

"Sounds like a tough assignment alright, not to mention an

emotionally charged one," she said. "You'd better brush up on your Creole."

"I've hired me a guide to help in that regard."

"Let's hope he's is a capable one and nothing gets lost in translation. Did you do a background check on him?"

"Nope. Didn't feel it was necessary. I'm trusting my instincts on this one. He did some work for me in the past and appeared a reliable fellow."

"Guide work?"

"No, he painted my office."

She gave him a puzzled glance.

"Yeah, he's a painter—a good one."

"When do you head out?" she asked.

"Monday. I got hold of the guide before I left, and he said he would meet me at my office first thing in the morning. He has a break in his schedule, so the timing couldn't be better for him."

"I should ask before we leave the interstate...have you had breakfast?"

"The one on the plane will do me. How about you?"

"I cheated while waiting for your flight and grabbed some coffee and a donut."

Adam reached across to pat her shoulder. "Clear evidence you're now a veteran cop," he said.

Carlita exited the interstate, steering the Jeep onto a parallel access road that several miles later intersected with the rural road that would lead them into the foothills.

"I'd say the driving conditions are considerably better than the last time you drove this road, don't you agree?" she asked.

"That's definitely an understatement," he responded, reflecting back to the whiteout conditions resulting in his getting lost.

After bobbing up and down over a succession of rising hills bordered by thick woods, they came upon a clearing, at which point Carlita pulled the Jeep to the side of the road. Off to their right, sitting about fifty yards back from the road, was the isolated cabin where

Adam, having lost his way in the storm, sought directions that fateful Christmas Eve. There to greet him was Noelle, a child of seven at the time, who was home alone and whose mother, unbeknownst to her, was hanging by her neck from a crossbeam in an adjoining woodshed. For Adam it began an intense homicide investigation that eventually led to the apprehension of a killer, not to mention a personal relationship with Carlita, a local detective assigned to the case. Above all, it led to the Christmas gift of a lifetime for him—the adoption of Noelle who had become a ward of the state, following the deaths of her mother and father, who later took his own life.

"Do you know if anyone is living there?" Adam asked, gazing at the familiar structure.

"I checked out of curiosity a while back. It's owned by an Italian couple who spend a few months out of the year here—Colorado's version of snowbirds. At the moment it's empty. Shall we take a closer look?"

"Why not," he said, cracking open the Jeep's passenger door and stepping out into the crisp morning air.

As they approached the cabin, Adam noticed the woodshed standing to the rear of the cabin where he had discovered Noelle's mother hanging by her neck. It was still intact from all outside appearances.

"I don't suppose you want to take a look in there," Carlita said, following his line of sight.

"That's one scene I don't care to resurrect," he said, returning his attention back to the cabin.

Carlita knocked on the front door as a precaution. As expected, there was no answer, so they focused on the small porch where two wooden deck chairs were positioned side by side. "Shall we?" she asked, motioning to them.

They settled in to savor the surrounding landscape, dominated by tall, tightly spaced spruce trees, stretching to the azure sky above. For several minutes they sat in silence, abandoning their senses to the sounds and scents emanating from the scene around them. Colorado at its finest, he thought, though it did little to ease his troubled mind.

"What is it Adam?" Carlita suddenly asked, ending the spell.

"What's what?" he lamely asked back, aware of a palpable tension in the air, caused no doubt by his obviously distracted mind.

"I'm a detective, Adam, as you well know. I consider myself a competent one, experienced in picking up clues, especially when they jump out at me, like when you gave me a hug instead of a kiss at the airport...when you decided to book a motel room rather than stay with me...when you made this such a quick trip...when you didn't bring Noelle along with you. Do you want me to go on?"

"No, that's not necessary," he said with obvious resignation. "To put it bluntly, Carlita, I'm struggling to summon up the courage to say what's on my mind, especially when my heart is not in it."

"Why don't I help you along?" she calmly said through the backdrop of birdsong coming from the trees. "Is there another woman?"

"Yes," he answered directly, following a brief pause. "Is it that apparent?"

She turned to him. "It's been seeping through your letters and our recent conversations," she said with a halfhearted smile. "Not that it matters now. What does matter is you traveled all the way here with the intention of telling me face to face and not copping out with a generic, impersonal letter. Still, the reality of it hits hard, Adam, even though it comes as no surprise," she said, tears streaming down her face. "For that I'm grateful, as I am for all the time we spent together."

Adam scooted his chair so that he was directly facing her. "I owe you so much, Carlita. Without you there would be no Noelle in my life, something I will never be able to repay you for."

"What you don't owe me is your love, Adam. It's not something I or anyone else can lay claim to. If you want to repay me, continue to be a good father to her," she said. "You once told me you believed it was divine providence that brought you here that Christmas Eve. Well, for what it's worth, I don't think there's any doubt about it."

"Noelle thinks so highly of you. She often talks about visiting you. I hope it's still a possibility."

"It's more than a possibility. She has a standing invitation, as do you. That is, if she doesn't mind you tagging along," she said, attempting to insert a little levity to the situation.

Adam looked into the distance. "You know, I've always liked bittersweet endings in the movies, like the one in *Roman Holiday*. On the one hand, I wanted Audrey Hepburn to bust out of her royal cocoon and rush off the stage into Gregory Peck's arms at the end of it. Now, I'm not so sure. I suppose that would have shattered the reality of the moment."

"That's the bitter part of it," she said. "The sweet part is the memory of all that came before it."

They lapsed back into a silence…two people seeking some solace and comfort in the wondrous view provided them from a tiny porch.

"Needless to say, the mood on this flight home is going to be nothing like it was when I first flew back with Noelle," he said, summoning up a much more pleasant memory in an effort to ease the gloom.

"You were floating on air, Adam. You didn't need a plane."

"For sure, and to top it off, it was her first flight. She was gripping my hand the entire way while gazing out the window."

"Even during your in-flight meal?"

"Even then. We each ate the meal with our one free hand. It is a good thing she is left-handed, or it would have made the task doubly difficult."

A sudden gust of cool air swept down the hillside, rustling the stately spruces, a reminder that winter would soon be upon the land.

"You know what I'd like to do right now, in fact, this entire weekend?" he asked.

"What's that?"

"Take long walks in these woods with you."

"Sounds like a good plan B," she said. "We sure won't run out of trails in these parts."

And so they walked and talked, and in-between laughed a little and sighed a little, and in the end realized they would always be able to maintain their friendship, which turned out to be no bittersweet ending at all.

———

Tamra glanced at the wall clock above her desk. She was about to call it a morning when Madison Davis strolled into the office.

"I came to pick up a document in my office and saw the light on in yours," he said. "Not a fun way for you to spend a beautiful Saturday morning."

"I needed to catch up on some preparatory work for Adam before he heads out of town."

"That's right...he's on the trail of a Mr. Coulter. Did he decide where he would begin his search?"

"Haiti is his starting destination. This Monday, as a matter of fact. Right now, he's up in Colorado but should be back by tomorrow night."

"Business trip?"

"No...social."

"Girlfriend?"

Tamra shrugged her shoulders as though it was of no concern to her.

"Mind if I have a seat?" he asked politely.

"No, help yourself," she said, powering down her computer and setting aside a stack of printouts.

"On the subject of social lives, when Adam came to my office to discuss his trip, I took the liberty of asking him what your social status was—single, married, whatever—and he said you were single but spoken for. I always found that phrase a little inexact so I thought I would take this opportunity to ask you directly. Are you spoken for?"

She knew, of course, where this was headed but given her current state of mind, she could use a little diversion. After all, he was a very good-looking guy and what woman would not welcome a little attention from him, if solely for the flattery of it?

"I've never cared for that designation, especially if it's referring to my social status," she replied. "It's as if someone other than me is speaking for me. Having said that, I do agree there is some truth in it when it comes to describing my current status. Is that confusing enough for you?"

He smiled. "'Some truth' you say."

"Yes…some."

"Adam told me he was an 'okay' guy…this anonymous boyfriend of yours."

She stifled a chuckle. "That's coming from a male perspective, but… yes, I would agree he's an 'okay' guy."

———

Yes, this woman is special, Davis thought. Ever since his arrival on the scene, it took but a few hallway chats with her to conclude it. As for her state of mind, he had seen them all in the course of his practice—the scorned woman, the betrayed woman, the woman on the cusp of a divorce, the battered woman, the burned-out woman—and particularly pertinent in this instance, the taken-for-granted woman. There was always the possibility she could be the one doing the taking for granted and not her beau, though in all likelihood, she was the one on the receiving end of it. Either way, it gave him his opening. He clasped his hands behind his neck and crossed his legs.

"Let me ask you, what do you do for recreation?"

"I spend most of my free time reading, when I'm not working."

"No outdoor physical activities? Swimming? Sailing? Jogging?"

"Up until a year ago, I played tennis regularly. I live right across from Greenfield Park where there are some nice courts. Friends accused me of moving there solely because of the courts."

"Why did you stop?"

"I lost my tennis partner. She moved out of town."

"What are you doing this afternoon?" he immediately asked.

"This afternoon? Well, Adam's daughter is staying with me while he is away but it so happens she's spending this afternoon over at her girlfriend's house," she said, opening the door for him.

Davis unclasped his hands from behind his neck, uncrossed his legs, and leaned in to grab the chance handed him. "I'm a tennis player. I have played at Greenfield Park several times. I'd like to meet you there at one o'clock for a friendly game. It's time for you to get back on the court, don't you think?"

He could see the debate raging in her mind. "It's a gorgeous day out there," he said, nudging her along.

"Okay, as long as you understand this is a tennis game, not a date," she stated directly.

"Agreed," he said, confident he had a foot in the door.

The moment Davis walked onto the Greenfield tennis court, the memories came flooding back to her. When she was a youngster growing up in the seventies, her mother signed her up for tennis lessons. From then on, she immersed herself in the game, not only in her personal development as a player, but as a fan of the stars of the sport, particularly one star…Björn Borg. The super-talented Swede with the long blond hair bound by a bandanna was a favorite of hers. She made sure she caught all of his televised matches. Like a groupie, she plastered her room with posters of him. It was said years previous that every woman in the country would have liked to have had one dance with Fred Astaire. How she would have liked to have had one game with the Swede! Madison Davis was no Björn Borg, but he would do for today.

"Before we begin, I need to take care of a little pregame business," he said, rummaging through his tennis bag. Moments later, he pulled out what appeared to be a tiny trophy. With a playful smile, he held it up for her to see. "Greenfield Park's Summer League Junior Championship runner-up trophy," he said, before placing it between them on a courtside bench they occupied. "It's intended to intimidate opponents," he added.

Tamra snatched a couple of sweat bands from her satchel and slipped them over her wrists. "I don't easily intimidate," she countered with a like smile, before stepping to her end of the court.

Turning to face him, she noted they were at least compatible in one regard. They both were wearing similar shades of powder blue shorts and tops. "Maybe a good omen," she mused. She had learned long ago that finding a good hitting partner was like finding a good dance partner. The goal was to establish a good rhythm with each other, which facilitated long rallies. After all, this was recreational, not competitive tennis. And as on the dance floor, she would bow to tradition and let him take the lead. Much to her delight, he did so with aplomb, quickly establishing a rhythm by accurately gauging the speed and placement of the ball that best suited her two-handed forehands and backhands. In no time, there emerged an uninterrupted flow to the exchanges of ground strokes that lasted nearly the entire afternoon, excepting a couple of errant ones by her, one of which toppled his trophy from its perch on the bench, drawing from him a feigned look of horror. Altogether, it made for a good workout, exceeding her expectations, and for the time being, taking her mind off of Colorado.

As for the psychologist, he knew he had brought out the best in her. The best for him was watching her toned and tanned body glide across the court in quick steps or long, sinewy strides to chase down his ground strokes. Never in his tennis experience had he seen a female hitting partner cut the figure she did on the court. At some point during the long exchanges, he must have traded in his analytical eye for an ogling one. It brought to mind the subject of his master's thesis— how to manage the carnal mind. Somewhere in the stacks of stuff in his office it lay. Maybe he should dig it out and reread his keys to controlling such thoughts. Yeah…sure, as though they could stand up to the vision of her stretching her fetching frame to launch a backhand.

"That was fun," she said at the end of the workout, words that virtually assured him a second outing. Needless to say, his goal to advance beyond tennis partner status with her was looking better, given the inroads he made on the court. Taking the next step to a personal relationship with her might call for more pushing of female buttons— deeply buried ones that he had become privy to over the course of countless patient therapy sessions. In the event the button pushing didn't work, he had a backup plan already in place involving her boss. Adam Fraley did not seem all that enthralled with Mr. Anonymous. He was convinced it wouldn't take much to persuade the P.I. to serve as his wing man in the pursuit of his office manager's affections.

———

Upon his arrival home from Colorado, Adam dialed his former boss and lifetime mentor Pete Peterson in the Florida Keys where he and his wife Jill were living out the remainder of their golden years. It was Peterson who got him started in the business and guided him through its intricacies during the early stages of his career, offering encouragement when needed and professional advice when warranted.

"I agree…the finding is the easy part," he responded on hearing Adam's summation of the Coulter case. "You'll have to come up with something better than 'Oh, forget about it' if you're planning to talk him off the island. Forgetting the incident is not an option for him in this instance."

"That's essentially what the therapist said to me."

"You got a therapist?"

"No, I don't. The complex we're in does. He moved his practice upstairs a short while back. Considering the psychological issues involved in the case, I thought it might be worthwhile to consult with him."

"My wife worked as an office manager for a psychologist in her younger days," Peterson pointed out. "She said you had to be prepared for the unusual in that job, and not only from the clients."

"Unusual in what way?"

"This guy told her right upfront there was no sense in reinventing the wheel when it came to dispensing psychobabble. 'Why throw a bunch of academic jargon at the clients when it's already been reconstituted down to their level of understanding by the nation's songwriters,'" he advised her.

"The nation's songwriters?"

"Yep, the guy instructed her to compile an extensive file of sheet music going back a half century. Her job was to organize and highlight any lyrics her boss might deem pertinent to the psychological disorders afflicting his clients."

"What sort of disorders?"

"Mostly depression arising from rejection, separation, betrayal, failure and the like. I told her she should have suggested he buy an old jukebox and hand the clients a roll of coins and a list of selections so they could have at it while he sat back and hummed along. By the way, do you remember the old song 'I'm Always Chasing Rainbows'?"

"Must have been before my time, Pete."

The answer didn't stop his mentor from launching into a sing-song voice. "'I'm always chasing rainbows, watching the clouds drifting by. My schemes are just like all my dreams, ending in the sky.' According to my wife, he'd pull that one out more than any other, claiming it represented a universal state of mind that showed just how normal it was to experience failure, no matter the effort one puts into avoiding it. We all suffer from pie-in-the-sky dreams, so why feel like a failure in life? That was his stock line, or should I say the songwriter's line."

"I assume the sheet music was placed in folders. He didn't just walk into a session waving them, did he?"

"No, Jill had them in folders so he could review the lyrics beforehand and make his selections so as not to give away any of his trade secrets. Her fear was that he would one day start singing the lyrics to the clients. She doesn't like behavior that makes her cringe…never has."

"And she's married to you?"

"Hey, I may have my idiosyncrasies but I'm not that strange."

"How long did she last at the job?"

"Long enough for me to come along and rescue her from it. I have often wondered whether it was the job or my charms that drove her into my arms."

"Now she's waiting for someone to come along and rescue her from you—right?" ribbed his former underling.

"I figure if that was going to happen, it would have by now, not after fifty years of marriage."

"What's the secret, "Pete?"

"Secret for what?"

"You two making a successful go at it."

"I'll give you the trite answer. You either have to grow together or you grow apart. There is no standing pat. Believe me...it's easier said than done."

"The psychologist I mentioned earlier has his eye on Tamra," Adam said straight out.

"What guy doesn't?" Peterson asked in a matter-of-fact manner. "Dare I say it...Tamra's not only the resident beauty but the backbone of Adam Fraley Private Investigations."

"Couldn't have put it better, Pete."

"How are you two getting along?"

"Fine...I think."

"You think? Well, how about the cop in Colorado? Where do you stand with her?"

"I don't anymore. I broke up with her."

"You mean you dumped her?"

"Hold on, Pete. You make it sound crude when it wasn't. No, she's a good woman and probably a far better person than I. We'll remain friends, for sure."

"'A far better person than I.' Where have I heard that one before? Oh, yeah, right after your last two breakups. It's becoming your standard throwaway line. Are you saying you can't measure up to a better class of women? I hope you're not feeding them that excuse. Comes across as very patronizing to me."

"No, it is not something I say to them, Pete. Give me credit for some sense. I'm sure as hell not going to tell them they're not the right woman for me. How many ways could that be misinterpreted?"

"The point is you might want to consider exactly what you mean when you say a far better person. At the risk of stepping into tender territory, maybe you should stop looking for far better women. They apparently are not suited to your taste, though you seem attracted to them. On the other hand, nabbing what you consider a step up in class might not be such a bad thing, especially with Noelle in the picture."

"If you're seeking a definition of what kind of woman I'm looking for, you won't get it from me. I'm not sure I could boil it down to a simple definition, nor do I wish to. As a matter of fact, I'd prefer her to be indefinable."

"I recall Carlita when she was doing the background check on you during your adoption of Noelle. She grilled me good. I was impressed. The tough part of it was having to say all those nice things about you," Peterson said. "All kidding aside, a tough thing for you, I'm sure, especially after hearing all the nice things you had to say about her over the years."

"What's tough is sustaining a long-distance relationship."

"Listen, some of the best marriages are those where one spouse lives in one state…say, Alaska…and the other in Florida. The harmony between them is great," he said, returning to the light side. "Domestic disturbances are rare in those situations."

"Estranged spouses are a different matter, Pete, as you well know."

"So how's Noelle?"

"She's a handful."

"Good," Peterson declared. "That girl's going to shake up the world one day, after she finishes shaking up yours, of course."

"Back to the case I'm on. Any other suggestions you might have?"

"You're traveling to Haiti on your own?"

"No. I have an acquaintance who lived and worked there for a while going with me. He speaks the language."

"All for the better. Overcoming the language barrier is the number one obstacle to surmount in any foreign ventures. The one other piece of advice I have is to press Coulter on the family issue. It's the surest lure you have in selling him on a return."

"That's also what the therapist suggested to me."

"Smart fellow. All the more reason to keep an eye on him when it comes to Tamra."

"Tamra can take care of herself."

"Oh, I definitely agree…for the time being."

"What do you mean…for the time being?"

"Who's to say if or when a person's defenses might crumble, even Tamra's, given the right circumstances, the right man, and the right words.

"Thanks for putting my mind at ease, Pete."

"Hey, that's what I'm here for, my friend."

"To sort out my love life?"

"To make sure you have one left to sort out."

"I have some breaking news for you, Pete. I'm done with the sorting."

CHAPTER FOUR

Tamra had just opened the front door for Monday morning business when Adam and Pierre Gantt arrived on the scene. All three immediately gathered around her desk for a pre-trip briefing. "Here is a list of Catholic churches and church-sponsored missions and orphanages I came up with," she said, handing Adam a file folder. "I also included the addresses and phone numbers of a few government agencies that might be of help. At your request, I did not include hotel and motel locations."

"Pierre tells me he knows of a conveniently located one that doesn't require reservations," Adam replied, nodding to the man standing beside him.

Pierre was of early middle age, a barrel-chested man of medium height and sturdy build with a large sloping head, thick neck, and broad shoulders. A bushy, rust-colored beard compensated greatly for his barren scalp. His husky voice perfectly fit his mountaineer image. "And it's reasonably priced and clean," he said, "unless it's completely fallen apart since I was last there."

Adam turned his attention to his office manager. "I called your place earlier this morning and talked to Noelle. You had already left. She's not giving you any trouble, is she?"

"Noelle? She's no trouble at all. We're having all sorts of fun while her father is away taking care of important business," she said, with a tinge of sarcasm.

Yep, Colorado is still on her mind, the recipient of the zinger figured. "Well, we'd better get going," he said. "I'll touch base with you once we learn something significant."

"You sure you don't want me to give you a ride to the airport?" she asked.

"No, you're needed here. Besides, we shouldn't be gone long. I'll just leave my car at the airport lot."

Adam took a step back to leave but stopped to lock eyes with his office manager. For what specific reason, he was at first unsure. A moment later he was sure. He didn't want to leave on a sour note. Meanwhile, Pierre's eyes darted back and forth between the two, sensing the unspoken. Aware of the unease, Tamra rose from her chair and in deliberate fashion walked to where Adam stood, slipping an arm around his neck and giving him a hug. "Be careful, and you also, Pierre," she added, glancing at his traveling mate.

———

"Okay, what the hell was that all about back there in your office?" Pierre asked on the way to the airport. "I sense a more personal vibe between the two of you since I was last here."

"You sense right," Adam answered straight out, as he navigated the heavy early morning traffic.

"Nice…I like your taste. She looks to be out of most guys' league."

"And maybe mine," Adam opined.

"Tell me, exactly how did you get so lucky? There must have been no shortage of suitors waiting in line to gain her attention."

"Actually, there were none. She had completely soured on men from what my daughter told me, particularly after a disastrous date of hers."

"How long ago was that?"

"Two or three years ago. For professional reasons I never made a point of probing Tamra's private life, like my daughter did."

"Your daughter ended up playing matchmaker for you?"

"For herself…she wanted a mother. Still does."

"Two or three years since her last date…must have been a doozy to cause that long of a hangover."

"From what I gather, it was her third straight dinner date with the guy. The first two apparently held out some promise for her. For openers he was exceptionally nice-looking and seemed pleasant enough. Secondly, he ran a successful roofing business he had built from scratch."

"So the first two dates earned the fellow a third, which led to what?"

"The truth," Adam said over the drone of traffic. "From what I understand, the guy without much of a hint suddenly morphed into a suffocating, overbearing boor, who attempted to pressure her into some kind of permanent relationship. 'I had given up hope on finding the right woman and then you came along to give me hope…you may be my last chance at finding love, Tamra.' Those sorts of lines that screamed desperation."

"Couldn't rein in his ardor, could he?"

"No, and because he couldn't, she was becoming desperate herself as to whether she was going to survive the evening with her emotions intact. Tamra is not one to suffer boors gladly."

"Women should always have an exit plan when in the early stages of dating, like 'I'm sorry, I've got to get up early in the morning to go to work' or 'I'm feeling very sick at the moment.' Hell, even the direct method, like 'We're not a match' or simply 'I have to go. It was nice meeting you.'"

"Though she doesn't stomach boors well, she also tries not to be rude. Besides, he was driving that evening. When all was said and done, she did the next best thing."

"And that was?"

"According to my daughter, after one of his pleas, she politely said, 'Will you please excuse me a moment, I need to make a visit to the ladies' room.' The answer to her predicament, it turned out, was mounted on the wall next to the restroom entrance. She pulled the fire alarm."

"Yes!" Pierre blurted out, slapping the dashboard. "Now there's a gal with grit who knows how to pull the plug on a bad date. I bet that turned the night on its head."

"It disrupted their dinner long enough for her to claim she was too distracted by what she did to continue with the date."

"What reason did she give for pulling the alarm? I assume she confessed to it."

"She did, claiming she saw smoke pouring from an adjoining room which turned out to be the kitchen, as she well knew. As dumb as it sounded, the manager bought her story, or at least accepted it."

"That ended the relationship with her suitor?"

"On the way home, she let it be known there would be no more keeping company with him."

"And thus started her self-imposed exile from the dating scene... worked out well for you, my friend."

"We'll see."

They sat at a stoplight not far from the airport, waiting for it to turn green.

"Are you married, Pierre?" Adam asked, at the turning of the light.

"For fifteen years, I was."

"Ended in divorce?"

"No...her death...seven months ago."

"Oh, sorry," Adam said. "Sudden?"

"No, she died of Hodgkin's Disease. The doctors said she had a genetic predisposition to being struck by it during her lifetime. It was prevalent in her family history."

"Were you aware of the history prior to your marriage?"

"She was upfront about it, told me of the risk involved, but I loved her and was more than willing to face it as long as she was."

"No children?"

"No, which may have been a blessing."

A brief silence ensued between the two. Pierre broke it with a reference to another weighty topic, one more pertinent to the matter at hand. "About this Coulter guy...what makes you think he will be willing to return to Florida?"

"The likelihood is that he won't be."

"How do you aim to convince him…that is, if we find him?"

"Convince…coerce…shame…bribe…kidnap…whatever works."

"He has not kept in touch with his family at all?"

"Not since he skipped out, according to his daughter."

"Hard to figure, considering how much of a family man you say he was."

"The pain of separation from his family is all part of his self-imposed penance. He may not admit it, but the incident preys on his spiritual fears. He's saturated with guilt. Who wouldn't be under those circumstances? He believes he's got the blood of a child on his hands… his own child. How much penance is that worth?"

"Whatever happened to three Hail Marys and three Our Fathers?" Pierre opined.

———

The flight from Tampa took them to Fort Lauderdale where in turn they boarded a flight to Port-au-Prince. Toussant L'Ouverture International Airport turned out to be a hive of activity. Long lines jammed ticket counters as arriving and departing passengers crowded boarding and arrival gates. Maneuvering their way through the foot traffic, Adam and his companion found a rental car station where they leased a late model Land Rover. The two soon discovered the chaos in the airport terminal was superseded by the chaos on the streets.

"The first thing you learn here is that the traffic signs are little more than suggestions," Pierre said from behind the wheel. "Drivers use whatever side of the road is open at the moment, especially on the rural roads. The second thing to remember follows from the first…keep out of the other fellow's way."

On Pierre's advice they decided to book a room at a hotel not far from the airport—the same hotel he stayed at while doing subcontract work in the country. By mid-afternoon, they had settled into their room, a tiny unit sparsely furnished with two beds, a small desk, a phone, a television, and shower. "Two-star," Pierre said. "Five-star for most Haitians," he added.

"Any last-minute advice on how to interact with the locals?" Adam asked.

Pierre chuckled. "Funny, you should ask," he said, picking through a worn briefcase of his and slipping out a small pamphlet. "Someone gave me this before I left," he continued, holding it up for Adam to see. "It provides basic advice on how to interact with the natives when on a temporary mission."

"Let's hear it," Adam said, sitting on the edge of his bed.

Pierre opened the pamphlet and began to read. "'One...Give the locals their personal space. Don't crowd them. Two...Don't complain about local mores. They'll tell you to go back to where you came from. Three...The great majority of residents are friendly. Welcome their friendship. Four...Even the deprived in the society are generous. Make a point of acknowledging their generosity. Five...There is a great zeal for life among the populace. Engage in it. Six...Generally, the locals are frank and direct with others. Respond in kind when appropriate.'"

Having completed his recitation, Pierre slipped the pamphlet back into his briefcase. "There you have it."

"Those sound more like American traits," Adam responded.

"They are...the guy gave me the wrong pamphlet," his traveling companion answered with a grin. "That was a guide designed for people who were assigned missions to the United States."

"I thought we sent missions out. I didn't think we brought them in."

"There are occasions when it occurs, particularly with those who aim to evangelize a portion of the populace."

"Back to my original question...any advice on interacting with the locals—Haitians, if you will?"

"You can't go wrong with the golden rule, Adam. It applies here as much as anywhere else on the planet."

Neither of them wishing to waste time, Pierre suggested they first take a quick trip to the Iron Market, a Haitian favorite, to pick up some food supplies. While there, they could start passing around the photo of Coulter to vendors. Adam concurred and off they went.

———

Engraved on the archway to the Iron Market were the words *Paix* and *Travail*—peace and work. Peaceful was not a word Adam would have used to describe the market. As Pierre forewarned on the ride over, it was more like two blocks of street vending bedlam. Contributing to the commotion were the strains of island music blaring in the background. Except for a few goats and chickens running about freely, Adam thought it resembled a typical flea market back home. The many food items on display made up a colorful palate of yams, carrots, cabbages, avocados, plantains, mangoes, grapefruits, peanuts, oranges, beets, meats, and fish. Adam let Pierre take the lead, following him from table to table as he exchanged greetings, perused the offerings, some of which he purchased with the gourds he had exchanged for dollars back at the hotel. As he did so, he deftly brought to the vendor's attention the photo of David Coulter, asking, "*Eske ou we?*"…Have you seen? It was a phrase Adam would come to hear repeated countless times during their journey. "*Non,*" the vendors all replied in quick fashion.

One display stand in particular caught Adam's eye. On it were rows of a brown, disk-shaped food item called *galette*…clay cakes, according to Pierre. "They're made from mud, butter and salt and baked in the sun. They're considered a delicacy among the impoverished, particularly during periods of widespread famine. For that reason, I'm a little surprised to see them in the Iron Market. It's not like they are in great demand at the moment."

"What do they taste like?"

"Let's just say they don't taste like chicken…more like cow pies… the barnyard ones," his companion quipped, squelching any temptation he might have had to sample one.

During one stage of their stroll, Adam asked of Pierre, "Is it me or does it seem Haitian men are averse to smiling? I have yet to see a single one coming from them, whereas the women burst into these beautiful big ones at the slightest attention given them."

"Must be your good looks turning on the women and turning off the men," Pierre cracked, edging his way through another cluster of customers.

"As my daughter often says to me when befuddled, 'get serious.'" Adam retorted. "Don't tell me you haven't noticed."

"I'd say it's more happenstance than cultural, my friend. Don't worry, I'm sure that first smile from a Haitian male is coming your way. My advice is to be prepared for it."

"What the hell does that mean?"

"It simply means not all smiles are genuine, here or elsewhere in the world. For every five hundred nice ones you get, there's always that sinister one to ruin a day."

By the time they had covered the two blocks of displays, the still air hovering over the proceedings had grown thick. Off in the distance, rolls of thunder drummed a warning of an advancing storm. Soon, the bright sun was giving way to dark, churning clouds that were about to turn day into night. As the booms drew closer, vendors scrambled to cover exposed merchandise. In short order, scattered drops of rain splattered against umbrellas and the dry ground, heralding what was to come. It was enough warning for the two to call it a day and head for the car.

Back in their hotel room, they agreed a fruit and vegetable dinner concocted from their haul at the market would suffice for their evening meal. They spread the foodstuffs on top of the desk...oranges, bananas, boiled peanuts, apples, carrots, and celery sticks. To complement the meal, Pierre pulled from a sack what he called the "pride of Haiti"—a bottle of cinnamon-flavored Haitian rum. "You've got to try this," he said, holding the bottle up for his roommate to see.

"I'm game," Adam said, holding out one of the two plastic cups he had earlier retrieved from atop a bathroom washbasin.

Pierre poured the liquor very carefully into the two cups, as if it was nectar from the gods. When finished, he raised his in a toast. "Here's to a successful hunt," he said, prompting Adam to respond in kind.

"Man, that's fine tasting stuff," Adam said, lowering his cup. "Let's hope the country doesn't run out of it."

"Don't worry. There's plenty more of it out there," Pierre said, munching on some peanuts. "A couple of bottles of the stuff and you'll be walking on your elbows."

"The perfect drink for circus clowns," Adam jested.

"By the way, do you notice anything familiar about this room?" Pierre asked.

Adam surveyed the surroundings. "Offhand, the only thing I notice is that the color scheme looks a lot like the one we have in our office back home."

Pierre grinned. "It's the exact same scheme—pastel yellow. I and a co-worker of mine painted this room. In fact, we painted every single room in this place," he exclaimed, waving his arms in every direction.

"Which explains the discount you got for the room," Adam said, nibbling on a celery stick.

"So, what do you make of your first day in Haiti?" Pierre asked.

Adam reflected a moment. "Well, I got a taste of the place and that's a start. As for the Iron Market, I suppose we shouldn't have expected much more. The fact none of the vendors recognized Coulter from the photo doesn't come as much of a surprise. I know we are trying to touch all bases, but the chances of him hanging out at a place like that were slim anyway. Don't you agree?"

"From what you have told me about him, I agree. The Iron Market is too much in the middle of things...too high profile."

Adam nodded. "Yeah, he's going to seek out a landing spot that falls under the religious umbrella," he ventured. "It's in his comfort zone."

"You mentioned on the flight over he was part of a couple of church missions here. Did you check with them?"

"Tamra contacted his church on that very matter. Turns out no one could recall an exact locale for the missions, though they seemed to think it was somewhere in the Cite Soleil district, one of the places on Tamra's checklist."

Pierre took a swig of the rum. "Oh yes...Cite Soleil...Port-au-Prince's slum of slums...the most dangerous neighborhood in Haiti," Pierre said. "On a positive note, it does represent a more likely landing spot for him, not to mention a fertile hunting ground for us."

"Let's make it our first stop tomorrow morning," Adam said.

"You're the boss," Pierre responded, finishing off an apple.

With a long day ahead, the two took to their beds early, the rum hastening their descent into a deep sleep.

CHAPTER FIVE

"WELCOME TO THE LAND OF THE HAVE-NOTS," PIERRE SOMBERLY announced from his driver's perch upon their arrival at Cite Soleil.

"What else do you expect from a country that's been crapped on through the years by politicians and nature alike," Adam noted.

The narrow road they had taken through the notorious slum was lined with long stretches of squalid tin shacks, tent cities, and crumbling, pock-marked concrete structures. Open sewers ran parallel to the roadway, emitting a putrid odor that permeated the air. Along the route skeletal stray dogs roamed freely in search of their next meal. Unlike much of what Adam had witnessed thus far on the trip, this was an urban landscape as drab and colorless as any he could recall. What wasn't colorless, however, were the flashing red and blue strobe lights mounted on the dashboard of a dark blue SUV that abruptly appeared on their tail.

"For God's sake, what's this all about?" Adam barked.

"Could be anything," Pierre replied, easing the Land Rover to the side of the road. "There's little police presence around here. Even the cops are reluctant to enter the area, which allows the gangs to run free for the most part."

Pierre lowered the driver's side window to greet the oncoming interloper, a squat little guy carrying a clipboard. He wore a mud brown shirt and shorts and a face empty of expression.

"Good morning," Pierre said, avoiding the Creole. Adam recalled his traveling companion mentioning how he on occasion would stick to English when the situation called for it. "Oftentimes it's advantageous to play the role of innocent tourist," he had claimed.

"You need follow me," the short guy said in broken English.

"Follow where?" Pierre asked.

"And what for?" Adam added from the passenger side.

"Just follow," the guy said in a restless voice, refusing further explanation.

Pierre glanced at Adam. "I suggest we do as he says," to which Adam replied, "you think?" but didn't protest further, believing it the prudent thing to do under the circumstances.

"*Pa gen pwoblem,*" Pierre said to the fellow, reverting for the moment to Creole.

The SUV led them further down the route they were on, before turning onto an even narrower side street that was badly in need of repair. "As though there was such a thing as road maintenance in this part of town," Adam whispered to himself. "Have any idea what this might be about?" he asked aloud.

"No idea. He could be representing anything from the undercover police to a drug cartel," Pierre said. "Should have known we would attract attention. Here we are, a couple of white guys cruising Cite Soleil in a late model Land Rover. It's not like we were the normal backpack-carrying church kids on an international aid mission. At least it's broad daylight," he then added, keeping the Land Rover close on the tail of the SUV.

"You mean the risk factor rises after dark," Adam said.

"Exponentially so," Pierre responded. "Doesn't it everywhere?"

As if things couldn't get any stranger, at that moment a motor scooter came roaring up from behind and immediately veered to pass them and the SUV. It wasn't just any motor scooter, though. This guy had mounted on the back of his vehicle a giant-sized flag, as big as any you would find on a car dealer's lot in the States. And not just any flag, but the Confederate flag.

"What the hell!" Adam exclaimed.

Pierre could not control his laughter, guffawing at the sight.

"Okay, mister guide, explain that one to me," Adam said, as the scooter passed, trailing high the stars and bars for everyone to see.

"The peasant class in this country is always making noises about rebelling against what they claim is constant government oppression. I'm guessing he was looking for a symbol of opposition and somebody, maybe a tourist, talked him into buying a rebel flag he was peddling."

"That wouldn't have been you by chance?" Adam joshed.

Pierre looked askance at his companion. "I'm a stars and stripes guy…always was and always will be."

"Good. What we don't need at the moment is to get caught up in a revolution."

"Agreed," Pierre said.

They motored on, driving past one decayed building after another, wondering which ones might be inhabited and by whom, and for what. In short order, the SUV veered off the road and pulled to a stop alongside a square concrete structure set back twenty yards from the street. It was similar in appearance to an automobile repair garage with a door-less, opened entrance on one end and an office on the other. The driver stuck his head out of the SUV's window and motioned to the building. "Somebody wait for you inside," he shouted out, and drove off.

They entered the office part where two stern-looking men—one bearded, the other sporting a mustache, stood on one side of a wooden table awaiting them. Both were dressed in what apparently was the uniform of the day—mud colored t-shirts and shorts. The table and a few straight-back chairs were the sole furnishings in the room, except for a lit table lamp whose cord ran from the table to a faraway wall socket. But for several random skid marks, the floor presented the same blank look. The walls were even more bare—no pictures, no graffiti, no shelves, no markings of any kind.

There were also no introductions, the bearded guy simply

motioning for everyone to have a seat at the table. In so doing, Adam noticed the man with the mustache nodding to Pierre. It was unmistakably a sign of recognition which immediately raised in Adam's mind the question of not how well the guy knew Pierre, but how well Pierre knew his greeter. Before Adam could begin to hash it all out in his mind, the bearded one opened a folder and slipped out four photographs and slid them across the table face-up for the two to look at. "Do you know them?" he asked in excellent English. They were photographs of four white guys, all with an American look to them. "No," each answered with a shake of the head. At this point, the mustached guy already appeared bored with the procedure, propping his elbow on the table and resting his face on his hand, an indication to Adam this was a rote exercise repeated several times a day.

In a trice, the bearded one quickly gathered the photos from the table like he would a losing hand from a card game and stuffed them back into the folder. "That's all," he said, abruptly ending the session.

"Wait...I have something for you to see," Adam said, before they had a chance to rise from their chairs. He plucked from his shirt pocket the photo of David Coulter and slid it across the table. "Recognize this guy?"

"No," said the bearded one, shaking his head. "No," repeated his partner, giving it a cursory glance.

With that, the meeting was over, that is, if you could call it a meeting, Adam mused. "Hell, they didn't even ask for our passports," he said, as soon as they were back on the road. "You have any inkling of what that was all about?"

"Drugs," Pierre answered directly. "Crack, along with everything else, is sold on the open street here. Those guys they were looking for were no doubt dealers. As for not asking for our passports, they really didn't give a damn whether we were here legally or not. They weren't about to be sidetracked from their primary mission, dealing in the drug trade."

"Dealing or receiving?" Adam pointedly asked.

"Your guess is as good as mine."

The image of the knowing nod the mustached guy gave Pierre still hung heavy on Adam's mind as the two settled into a silence. Intuitively, he sensed it was also on his compatriot's mind. After all, it was there for everyone in the room to witness.

Pierre momentarily took his eyes off road to cast a glance at Adam. "You caught that back there, didn't you?" he asked.

"Caught what?"

"Come on…the nod the mustached guy gave me," Pierre said, abruptly steering the Land Rover around a couple of large potholes, kicking up a cloud of dust as he did so.

"How could I not? Friend of yours?"

"No, he's actually a brother in arms to you."

"Care to explain?" Adam asked, flummoxed by the reference.

"He's a private investigator, or at least he was when I was working here. The hotel we're staying at was having a problem with employee theft, so apparently, they hired the guy to investigate it. I was among the guests he interviewed."

"You were robbed?"

"Nope, but the fellow in the next room was. I'm not sure if they ever did nab the perpetrator. If they did, they didn't bother to let us know."

"So the mustached guy is working for whom now?" Adam asked.

"Your guess is as good as mine. Whatever they're up to, I think we can safely assume it has nothing to do with our mission." Pierre again glanced Adam's way. "Say, maybe you should open up a branch office here in Haiti. You can bet the assignments would be much more adventuresome than tracking down cheating spouses back home."

"It's not a cheating spouse we're after, Pierre. It's a family deserter."

"Ah…a deserter you say…someone who has withdrawn from life's struggles and has no intention whatsoever of returning to the battlefield," Pierre waxed aloud. "Should be interesting."

––––––––

Although she was uncertain of its accuracy, the address of the Catholic mission Tamra had given Adam and Pierre turned out to be the correct one. The entire compound was surrounded by a low-level, perimeter fence. Inside stood a church adjacent to a school. While of greater size, both were typical of the bland, crumbling concrete structures characteristic of Cite Soleil. The sole distinguishing feature between the two buildings was a cross mounted above the church.

Pierre swung the Land Rover through an open entrance way. He pulled it to a stop in proximity to the school where clusters of students, dressed in parochial school uniforms, mingled about, evidently waiting for class to begin. Immediately, a number of the kids surrounded their vehicle in what already had become a familiar and endearing experience on their journey…hopeful children with smiling faces and outstretched arms, seeking anything from a handout to a moment of attention.

They hopped from the car into the milieu of children. "*Pret! Pret! Pret!*" Pierre called out to them. At once their outstretched arms turned and pointed in unison to a tall, lanky man sporting a baseball cap who was talking to a woman near the entrance to the school.

"That must be the pastor," Pierre said. "Why don't you go talk to him while I entertain the kids."

"Entertain them with what?"

Pierre reached into his back pocket and pulled out a deck of cards. "With these," he said, fanning them with a single upraised hand. "Don't leave home without them…something I learned early on while working here. Kids in this country are no different from those everywhere. They love tricks."

Adam slipped through the pressing crowd of children and walked over to where the priest stood. On seeing his approach, the clergyman, donned in jeans, faded blue t-shirt, and sandals, broke off his conversation with the woman who turned and entered the school.

"I understand you are the pastor," Adam said with outstretched hand.

The clergyman took his hand, displaying a firm grip. "You understand correctly," he said in a friendly but coarse voice that was distinctly American…New England English to be precise. "What can I do for you?" he asked, releasing Adam's hand.

He related his reason for being there, sticking to the pertinent points to speed matters along.

"In other words, you're here to help fix a family, not a country," the priest said through a half smile. "Not the usual fare around here."

"The latter is definitely beyond my job description, not to mention my talents," Adam replied as he slipped Coulter's photo from his back pocket and handed it to the priest. "Here's a photo of the man in question."

The clergyman studied it for a moment. "Sorry, don't recognize him," he said and handed the photo back.

"Any suggestions as to where we might look?"

The priest shook his head. "You must realize that everything here in regard to aid relief is project centered. Groups come in, set up their tents, dispense whatever services they provide, and then leave. There is very little coordination on our part. We assume they are legitimate simply by their presence. Someone in the government or church hierarchy had to have given them clearance. It's not like they're here to bilk the locals out of their belongings, since they have few to begin with. Anyway, from what you tell me, this man does not sound like the kind of guy who would hook up with an organization, considering his state of mind. It seems to me he would more likely travel an independent path...seek out an isolated environment to lend a helping hand...or perform his penance, as you say."

"You don't provide accommodations for the aid volunteers here?" Adam asked.

"We are able to accommodate the small staff we have, but not the help from overseas. Many of the aid groups put their people up in resort hotels along the southern coast. Some of the volunteers end up feeling a little guilty staying at a four or five-star hotel overnight while the people they are here to assist are mired back in their usual poverty. Don't get me wrong. Their efforts are greatly appreciated. Every little bit helps. What we try to do here is in the same vein...give the kids a break from their harsh world, while at the same time providing them some hope in the form of a basic education."

The two lapsed into a silence, their attention drawn to the clamor of the children surrounding Pierre and his impromptu magic show.

Moments later, the pastor glanced at his watch and exhaled a deep breath. "Well, time for the start of school," he said, signaling the end of their little chitchat. "I do hope your Mr. Coulter finds his peace of mind, Mr. Fraley, whether it be here or elsewhere."

"So do I," Adam replied, "but first we have to find him."

Adam turned to leave.

"Mr. Fraley!" the priest called to him, momentarily halting his departure. "As you go about, remember this about Haiti...rich in love, poor in possessions."

Adam nodded. "I'll keep that in mind, Father."

———

"Where now?" Pierre asked, drumming his fingers on the steering wheel as they sat in the parking lot.

"Jacmel...Les Cayes...where are these towns?" Adam asked, reading from Tamra's contacts list.

"Not far from here...they're cities along the southern coastline of the country. Remember, this is a compact country."

"Not that I'm in a hurry, but do any of these towns have airports?" Adam asked.

"A select few, mainly those cities catering to the tourist trade. I'd describe them as airstrips—one-vending machine operations, except most of them don't even have that."

"Thankfully, our stay here will be a short one, or else my island fever may kick in," Adam let out.

"You an open road guy?"

"Definitely...I don't like continually running into stop signs in the form of a sea."

Adam glanced at the checklist. "According to Tamra, there are church missions located in both Jacmel and Les Cayes."

"Well, we have the remainder of the day to check them out."

"Let's do it," Adam said, "though I'm beginning to wonder if this mission of ours is nothing more than a shot in the dark."

"Still early in the game," Pierre replied, attempting to instill a little confidence in him.

The road to Jacmel was narrow, winding, hilly, and lined in stretches with thick vegetation. So severe were the numerous hairpin turns, Pierre would tap the horn prior to taking them as a warning to any oncoming vehicles. As with the other Haitian roads they had traveled thus far, old school buses painted in kaleidoscopic bright colors frequently populated the pathway, as did the ever-present motor bikes darting in and out of traffic. Nonetheless, the road overall was substantially less chaotic than those in the capital, Adam noted.

"This path we're on serves as a sort of demarcation line between the privileged class on the one side and the downtrodden on the other with no class in the middle," Pierre explained.

"I take it the tourist trade has a great influence in that regard?"

"Yep, the shoreline off to our left is where the upscale hotels are located. They give Jacmel and Les Cayes a step up in class. Jacmel also has many old, ornate mansions built by coffee producers that provide it an extra charm."

"To the right of us?"

"A more rural, mountainous region. The steep hills you see off to the right slope down to the shoreline. When Hurricane Gordon hit almost two years ago, there was a lot of slipping and sliding of mud and houses alike. Both Jacmel and Les Cayes got more than 12 inches of rain. A lot of the devastation was blamed on deforestation. The rainwater washed down the bare mountains unobstructed, sweeping along with it a number of shanty towns. Tens of thousands of people were left homeless in the storm's aftermath, which explains the continued presence of the church missions. The recovery is still not complete. I fully expect when it is, another storm will hit. That's life in Haiti."

Yet, despite the presence of the missions, it turned out the treks to Jacmel and Les Cayes were no more productive than the visit to Cite Soleil. Mission workers without exception gave no hint of recognition when Adam passed around the photo of Coulter. Not a one gave it a second glance. All of a sudden, he felt like the marathon runner who had "hit the wall" halfway into his race, struggling for a second wind to carry him to the finish line. Sure, it had happened before in cases of his when clues or breaks did not come his way early on, but then out of the blue one would occur, and he'd gain a second wind. Still, with every shake of the head from an aid worker or resident, he slowly became convinced the course they were following was an errant one. As the priest back in Cite Soleil suggested, Coulter likely was traveling an independent path. Finding an isolated environment in which to serve out his penance was more in keeping with his intentions. Operating in proximity to Haiti's "Gold Coast" would more likely serve as a distraction rather than an attraction to him.

"I have a suggestion," Pierre said toward the close of the day, no doubt sensing Adam's burgeoning frustration.

"No better time for one than now. What do you got?"

"It's probably something I should have suggested in the beginning. Why don't we hit the Haitian government offices in the morning to see if there is anything in the official records that might give us a clue to his whereabouts?"

"Sounds like a sensible plan," Adam said, welcoming the idea of a course correction.

CHAPTER SIX

MANY OF THE HAITIAN GOVERNMENT OFFICES WERE LOCATED along the Boulevard Harry S. Truman that ran through the center of Port-au-Prince. However, it was a U.S. Government office that ended up changing the entire course of Adam's investigation. It so happened the drive downtown at one point took him and his companion past the American Embassy, located in a historic gingerbread-styled building on the Champs de Mars.

"A quaint little place," Adam observed.

"Yeah, today it appears peaceful, but it can turn into a fortress quickly in times of turmoil, something there's plenty of around here," Pierre said, surveying the scene from the driver's seat. "Say Adam, I'd like to propose another correction to the course correction."

Adam chuckled. "If we keep this up, we're going to end up traveling in circles. Go ahead...what is it?"

"Seeing the embassy, it hit me. I know a guy who works in the place. His name is Armand Navarro. I met him while I was doing contract work here. Our top boss had arranged to have an embassy representative talk to the job crews about the do's and don'ts of life in Haiti for foreign workers. The rep was Armand. It turned out he also was from Louisiana's Creole country. I later ran into him a couple of times while out and about, once in a bar where we spent some time reminiscing about life on the bayou. It might be worthwhile to pay him a quick visit while we're here."

"To see if the name David Coulter ever crossed his desk?"

"His desk or a desk of someone else in there," Pierre said.

"Sounds like another sensible plan," Adam said, "though it might be time to follow through on one before we go to the next."

Pierre swung the car to the side of the embassy, finding an empty parking spot on the street. Inside, the building did not reflect the relatively peaceful atmosphere of the outside. A long line stretched from a front lobby reception desk. The chatter emanating from those waiting in it reverberated off the walls.

"I suppose we should follow protocol and get in line," Pierre said.

Adam nodded his agreement and the two took their place in the queue to wait their turn.

"Expect the unexpected" was no less a truism in the private investigation business than it was in most other professions, Adam believed, catching out of the corner of his eye a figure across the lobby walking toward the exit. "See that white guy in the maroon shirt and jeans with a Friar Tuck haircut headed for the exit?" he said to Pierre.

"I see him."

"I know this is not part of the plan, but can you do a quick tail of him to see where he might be headed? I'll explain later. Chances are I'll still be in this line when you get back, as slow as it's moving."

"Sure," Pierre said, breaking from the line to hustle after the guy.

Twenty minutes later, Pierre was back. Adam had advanced to the third spot in line when he was rejoined by his cohort.

"Were you able to find out anything?"

"A bit. He's driving a rental car…blue Chevy sedan. I followed him a few blocks to a motel. He headed straight to a room without stopping at the office, which leads me to believe he already had checked in."

"Unless, he was visiting someone else," Adam suggested.

"What's this all about?"

"His name is Colby Flint. He's a Tampa Bay-based private investigator."

"A competitor of yours?"

"You could call him that. As for what it's all about, it doesn't take much guesswork to conclude why he's here and it's certainly not to take in the sights."

"The Coulter case?"

"You bet. It's far from a coincidence he would show up about the same time as we do."

"Does he know you?"

"The P.I. community is a close-knit one, so it's not unusual for members to cross paths frequently, mainly at court hearings and occasional seminars. He's known to work on the edge of the law by taking on shady clients."

"Don't most P.I.'s work on the edge of the law?"

"Yes, but he's gotten close enough to it to be nicked a few times and have his license suspended. I'm guessing he's working for a lawyer hired by Mrs. Coulter's beau to conduct a sham search for her husband just to meet the requirement to have him officially declared dead or missing."

"Where do you fit in?"

"Good question. A better one is, how did they know to come to Haiti? I doubt they were tipped to it by Coulter's daughter or her mother."

"What do you suppose Flint was doing here in the embassy?"

"No doubt fishing for the same kind of information we're fishing for."

They were next in line when the call came not from the clerk behind the counter but from a man roaming the main hallway. "Pierre! What brings you here?"

Approaching them was a pudgy, baby-faced thirty-something fellow dressed in a crisp, short-sleeved lavender shirt and yellow tie.

"Armand! Just the man we were looking for," Pierre replied, extending his hand in greeting. Following a brief introduction to Adam, he got right to the point. "What we need, my friend, is help in finding a missing person."

"A Haitian?"

"No...an American."

"Okay, why don't we go back to my office and you can give me the details," he said, motioning them to follow.

They trailed him down a hallway to a small office with room enough for a desk and a couple of guest chairs. The cream-colored walls were bare except for a large purple and gold Louisiana State University banner pinned to the panel behind his desk.

"How are the bayou Tigers doing this year?" Pierre asked, as he and Adam settled into the chairs.

"Doing great until we met the Gators last weekend...took our first loss of the year."

Armand leaned back in his desk chair and folded his arms. "So, you're looking for a missing person...an American. You think he's somewhere in this country?"

Pierre deferred the line of questioning to Adam. "We have reason to think so," Adam replied.

"His name and where he's from in the States?"

"David Coulter. He's from Tampa, Florida."

Armand reached for a pen and piece of note paper to scribble the info down.

"How long has he been here?"

"Several years...probably around five or so."

"And you have no idea where in the country?"

"Correct."

"Have you contacted any of the Haitian government agencies?"

"No...we thought we'd start with you."

"Well, let's see if we can come up with something," Armand said, angling his chair to punch on a desk computer.

The two visitors waited patiently as the embassy worker alternately typed in the commands and browsed the results. A few minutes later, he paused, his eyes fixed on the screen. "Well, he does have a valid passport, if this is the David Coulter you are referring to," he said, turning the monitor so they could view the passport photo. "Is that him?"

57

"That's him," Adam replied.

"Let's see if he has a resident permit," Armand said, returning to his search.

"What's a resident permit?" Adam asked.

"It permits a one-year stay as opposed to the three-month allowance of a passport. However, I'm not seeing one," he said, attentively scanning the monitor. "That may not come as a surprise, if he's trying to conceal his whereabouts. Is that the case?"

"Yes, he's gone into hiding."

"From the law?"

"No, from his family."

"For nefarious reasons?"

"No, for personal," Adam replied deliberately, leaving it at that.

"Whatever the reason, I can understand why he would not take out a resident permit. It requires much more background information, including the location of his residency while in Haiti."

"Does this mean he's illegally in this country…that is, if he's here at all?" Adam asked.

"Not necessarily. There are many foreigners, especially from the States, who for one reason or another jump back and forth based on the passport limitation. At the end of three months, they will fly home and then return for another three months. They feel this gives them more freedom of movement and takes them out from under the constant eye of the host country."

Armand turned his attention back to the computer. "There is one other entry indicated for Mr. Coulter. Let's see what this is," he said, clicking the mouse.

For a minute or two, Armand studied the screen, his face absorbed by what he was seeing. Finally, he glanced back at his two visitors with a dumbfounded look in his eyes. "Well fellows, I'm not sure how this will hit you, but according to the document I'm looking at, your Mr. Coulter was declared deceased as of November 1994."

"Deceased?" the two responded in tandem.

"Where are you getting this from?" Adam quickly followed.

"Whenever there's a death of a foreigner in this country, in this case an American, Haiti's Civil Registry sends over to us a copy of the official Foreign Death Certificate. It's written in Creole."

"Does it list the cause of death?" Adam asked.

"Accidental drowning. It was issued on November 29, 1994."

"Not long after Hurricane Gordon," Pierre pointed out.

"Right...nearly a thousand Haitians were killed in the storm, many by drowning," Armand said.

"Which begs the question...why didn't his family know about it?" Adam asked. "Do the authorities not notify them?"

"That's left up to us," Armand said, "but we have to rely on the information provided to us on the death certificate. All it has on it, other than his name and home town, is a mailing address. A note has been attached indicating a copy of the certificate was sent to a doctor by the name of John Warnick in Tampa, Florida."

"Excuse me, may I borrow a pen and piece of paper?" Adam asked.

Armand slid a pen and slip of paper across the desk. "I'd make a copy of this for you, but my printer is down."

"What address does it give for Warnick?" Adam asked.

"It doesn't. It gives the address of an organization in Tampa he apparently works for or is associated with in some way."

"The name of the organization?"

"Overseas Missions United."

"And that's where they sent it?"

"Looks that way. It could be they were not able to find an address for the family so they sent it in care of this outfit."

"Do they have an address or phone number for the organization?"

"Just a post office box."

"That's okay...the organization's name will do for now," Adam said. "What else is on the certificate? Does it give any burial info?"

Armand glanced back at the monitor. "No...that is usually left up to the family. If the family requests assistance regarding the transfer of the body, we will try to accommodate them. The name of the physician certifying the death is listed on here, if you're interested."

"Yes...who is it," Adam asked, reaching for the pen.

"Vincent Perone."

"Do you have any idea who he may have worked for?"

"No. Somebody connected to the Civil Registry or Ministry of Foreign Affairs, I presume."

"Any way of contacting him?"

Armand shrugged his shoulders. "I can give the Civil Registry a call right now, if you like."

"Please," Adam said.

Armand checked his contacts file and dialed a number. A moment later he was conversing in Creole with whomever answered. Following a short discussion, he passed on what he had learned. "Mr. Perone is no longer working with the government. He quit about five months ago."

"Did they give a reason?" Adam asked.

"I asked that, and the answer was no. He just picked up and left."

"How authentic are these death certificates, Armand?" Pierre asked.

"I'd be lying if I said they were authentic without exception. I don't mean to speak ill of the host country's practices, but it's well known that scams can run rampant here, particularly during times of turmoil when confusion reigns. Documents can be fraudulently manufactured, especially if there's money being passed under the table. It may come as no surprise to you that insurance detectives from the States are constantly contacting us regarding a foreign death certificate's authenticity. It's become a cottage industry for them. Their goal is to bring the supposedly dead back to life." Armand shrugged his shoulders. "Who's to say your Mr. Coulter didn't have a hand in the making of his own death certificate? A clever attempt to bring a missing person search to a screeching halt, don't you think?"

"The only way I'll believe that is if his fingerprints are found on the document," Adam declared.

"Would you have any idea who on your staff handled the notification?" Pierre asked.

"No," Armand said. "I can tell you that the normal practice when we receive one of these certificates is to simply notify the contact listed on the document. I assume in this case it was someone at Overseas Missions United who was notified…someone who was either a next of kin or a legal representative who then took it from there."

"Providing you direction as to what to do with the body," Adam suggested.

"Right…if there was a body to begin with," Armand replied, reiterating his own doubt on the authenticity of the certificate.

"And to think the family has no knowledge of this whatsoever, fake or otherwise," Pierre said, throwing up his hands.

"One other question, if you don't mind," Adam said. "Have you ever heard of a man by the name of Colby Flint?"

"Never heard of him," came the firm reply. "Do you want me to check on him also?"

"If you don't mind," Adam said.

They waited patiently as Armand searched the computer again.

"The only thing we have on him is that he has a current passport. Is he someone you're looking for?"

"No, he's looking for us," Adam replied, prompting a look of befuddlement on Armand's face.

"If anyone asks, tell them we're off to parts unknown," Pierre interjected.

His friend grinned. "Parts unknown…I'll remember that in case someone does ask."

Adam offered his thanks to Armand and turned to his companion. "I suggest we hit the road and take some time to digest what we've learned."

"Right…and decide on a new course once again," he replied, a note of resignation in his voice.

———

"Here's an idea, Adam, why don't we take turns sitting in the Tampa airport every day for three months and monitor all of the incoming and outgoing flights to and from Haiti?" Pierre asked, sipping on a glass of Haitian rum in the comfort of their hotel room.

"Come to think of it, that might not be a bad idea. It wouldn't surprise me if Coulter did take the passport option. Calls for a lot of travel, but privacy is important to him."

"So where would he go…what would he do…to kill the time away from the overseas penance regimen you believe he's committed to?"

Adam was lounging on his bed, his hands clasped behind his head. "If he was the average guy on the lam, I could picture him sitting in a rental car on the street where his daughter lives, doing a little surveillance from afar, watching her coming and going for the pure joy of it. I can't imagine going long stretches of time without seeing my daughter."

"Or speaking to her."

"That's the penitent in him at work."

"You ready to put my plan in action then on the chance he might be doing a little surveillance of his family?"

"I believe he's completely isolated himself from them, Pierre. As for getting around the passport time limitation, he could be hopscotching back and forth to Puerto Rico or the U.S. Virgin Islands for all we know."

"Okay, so what's the better alternative?"

"The death certificate, fake though it may be, gave us a potential lead to follow through on. I'm going to give Tamra a call and ask her to check out this Overseas Missions United outfit and John Warnick, in particular."

"I can always give Armand a call, ask him if he could track down for us the person in the embassy who dealt with Flint. Whoever it was might be able to give us a clue to what he was up to."

"I think we milked Armand for as much information as we could. No doubt there are lines of confidentiality he must be careful not to cross. For now, let's be grateful for what he did give us. If need be, we can return for a follow-up."

Adam called his office manager to brief her on their findings. "Do you think we should contact Carolina or her mother to see if they know anything about the death certificate?" she asked.

"Not yet," Adam advised, "not until we confirm it one way or the other. How's my daughter getting along? She's not giving you any trouble, is she?"

"None whatsoever. She's still looking forward to our evening out with Bobby. I don't need to tell you she's very nervous about it."

"You mean she's nervous about how I'm going to handle it...right?"

"Right, though I assured her you would be on you best behavior."

"Are you sure of that?"

"No, not at all...I fibbed to her."

CHAPTER SEVEN

THEY DECIDED ON AN EARLY LUNCH, WALKING TO A CORNER CAFE a short distance from the hotel where at Pierre's urging, they each ordered a plate of fried chicken over a bed of rice and beans. "It's a staple of Haitian cuisine," he explained. When finished, they returned to their room to decide on the next step in their search, a decision made easy by the contents of an envelope that had been slipped under their door while they were away.

Adam retrieved the envelope, addressed on the outside to F-R-A-L-E-E in a scribbled handwriting. He slipped from inside it a sheet of paper with a single sentence scratched on it...in Creole, he presumed. "I'm in need of a translation," he said, handing it to Pierre who quickly provided him one. "If you're looking for Coulter, come to the steps of the Sans Souci Palace at eight o'clock tonight—alone."

Pierre checked the reverse side of the note to see if there by chance was further explanation.

"What do you make of it?" Adam asked.

"Not much...what about you?"

"One thing's for sure...all those people we were flashing Coulter's picture to who gave it not a second glance...well one of them sure as hell recognized it."

"And alerted an interested party," Pierre added.

"You bet and had someone slip us this note."

"Flint, maybe?"

"Possible. I am convinced he, as well as the other conspirators, now knows where we are. Yeah, the pot's been stirred alright. All of a sudden, we're not only the hunters but the hunted as well."

"And the same can be said of them."

"Yes, except they don't want Coulter to be found, at least by us, which means we need to look out for our backsides."

"Suppose they do find him first?"

"Not good for him or for us."

"The race is on, then."

"Looks that way," Adam said. "I think it best we operate on the assumption it is. Incidentally, where's the Sans-Souci Palace and do you know how to get there?"

"Yeah, I know where it is. I traveled there on a sight-seeing excursion with a few friends while I was working here. It's in the high country near Milot, a rural town near the northern shoreline of the country. The palace itself is in ruins...hollowed out by time."

"A shell of its old self, you're saying."

"Definitely, though it remains a popular tourist destination."

"Who lived there?"

"Some king named Christophe. He was a former slave who later became a leader in the country's revolution against France. It was the first and only successful slave revolt in the world, I might add. If you travel a little farther north of the palace, you'll hit on another historic landmark of the country...the Citadelle. It's a mountaintop fortress overlooking the Atlantic. It was built by the government to ward off any French attempt to take back the country. The structure is huge...shaped like a damn battleship. From a faraway enough distance, you would think it was Noah's ark perched on a mountaintop following the flood."

"How did they get the building materials up there?"

"On the backs of the workers. They had to drag huge stones up the mountain."

"How long a drive is it to the palace?"

"Three and a half to four hours, if everything goes well." Pierre glanced at his watch. "We have plenty of time to make it."

"Hey, it's not like we have anything better to do today."

———

The road north took them into Haiti's high country where green-sheathed slopes rose steadily up to pine-capped mountain peaks. Along the way they kept an eye out for a blue Chevy sedan, in case Flint decided to tail them. To Pierre it was the least of their worries. "I know the roads here. He doesn't," he confidently stated. "If he does show up on our tail, I can easily lose him."

"Maybe he also has a guide," Adam said, tongue in cheek.

Pierre flashed him a grin. "You're kidding right?"

Adam chuckled. "'Skin' would be an appropriate middle name for him, from what I hear of his spending habits."

"Are his smarts as skinny as his wallet?" Pierre asked.

"No, and that could be a problem."

On a couple of occasions Pierre pulled the car aside a natural overlook so they could take in the astonishing view of Gonave Bay's turquoise waters far below. The great bay's basin was rimmed by breaking surf, palm-fringed beaches, and the crab-like claws of the northern and southern peninsulas extending out from the mainland. Beyond the bay, brightly-hued sailing boats could be seen skimming silently over a blue-green Caribbean Sea that stretched to the horizon. Haiti, the two agreed, was an eruption of colors, no better appreciated than when viewing it from high above.

"The air's much cleaner out here in the rural areas," Pierre pointed out, "not as much technology, electricity, and congestion to foul the atmosphere as there are in the cities."

"Pretty much how it works everywhere...does it not?" Adam opined.

Once back on the narrow, winding road, Pierre returned to his precautionary horn-tapping as they approached every sharp curve. "If this was a straight-line route, we could probably be there in half the time," he observed. As they neared Milot, the road became more crowded with motor bikes zipping in and out of traffic, cars parked alongside the street at odd angles, street vendors hawking food stuffs and keepsakes of every kind, and pedestrians bearing wicker baskets of supplies atop their heads.

"How do those women manage to balance those loads on top of their heads?" Adam wondered aloud.

"Years of practice, my friend," Pierre said. "It's both a science and an art, learned by doing."

There was no city limits sign, though the increased congestion was sign enough they had reached the city. "We'll need to cut clear through the town to get to the palace on the northern end of it," Pierre advised. "Many of the tourists take a tap-tap from here on up, but the day is pretty much done for the tourist business."

"What's a tap-tap?" Adam asked.

"They're those gleefully decorated buses you occasionally see."

"Gleefully?"

"Gleefully...loudly...gaily...boldly...take your pick. You have to admit, the art work on them is unique. Reminds me of the tie-dye days."

"How did they come up with the name tap-tap?"

"Simple...when passengers want to get off, they tap-tap."

Following a stop-and-go ride through the congestion, they reached the far edge of town where the din of the streets began to fade into the background. Night had fallen and with it came a chill in the air, along with a welcome quiet. In the distance the hills had turned a deep purple. Pierre eased the Land Rover to the side of the road, cut the engine, and glanced at his watch. "We're a little early," he said.

"Is that it?" Adam asked, pointing up the slope of a mountain to the ruined shell of a building rising nearly four stories. He lowered his window to get a better look. The combination of moon glow and ambient light gave the structure a ghost-like appearance.

"That's Sans-Souci Palace, or what's left of it," Pierre replied. "Looks like a squared Halloween jack-o-lantern, doesn't it?"

"Built with masonry instead of pumpkin."

"Yep, originally built of masonry and covered with stucco."

"Where in the hell is that drumming coming from?" Adam asked, the pounding pulling his attention away from the palace to the surrounding environs.

Pierre chuckled. "Someone nearby is having a voodoo gathering… maybe in his or her backyard."

"You serious?"

"Dead serious. It's not like it's unheard of around here," Pierre stated with certainty. "It's all orchestrated by a voodoo priest. People begin to dance to the beat of the drums until they're driven into a frenzy. Many of them paint their face white to mimic the paleness of death. The moment the drumming stops, all collapse onto the floor and are considered possessed by some random spirit or god." He flashed Adam a sinister smile. "At this very moment there's a good chance an old woman is sticking pins in a wax figure of you. Once she's finished, they'll drink the blood of a slaughtered goat and mark the wax figure's head with the blood." Pierre turned to face his companion. "Maybe we should have consulted a medium before we took this on," he deadpanned.

Adam surveyed the scene, looking for other signs of life. "Any security around here?" he asked, drawing another chuckle from his companion.

"Virtually none, I would guess. Oh, there might be an occasional unmarked patrol car making an appearance, but there's really nothing to steal up there and vandalism is out of the question. Haitians revere this place. The perimeter fence you see can be easily scaled, or if you prefer, look for a section with gaps in it."

Pierre again glanced at his watch. "Appointment time," he said. "You sure you don't want me to tag along with you?"

"No, we'll abide by the terms, but if I'm not back in twenty minutes, come looking for me."

"Well then, you might keep this in mind…*sans souci*…it means without worry," Pierre said, giving his sidekick a good luck tap on the shoulder.

Adam hopped from the car, found a gap in the fence, and commenced his hike up the steep hill, accompanied by the pulsating beat of the voodoo drums borne across the landscape by a light tropical breeze. Along the way he spotted a small domed church sitting off to the side of the grounds, a structure he presumed once served as a chapel for the royals. To his right was a large garden that fronted the palace. Nearing the shadowy edifice, twin flights of steps leading up to a portal landing came into view. Neither the steps nor the landing were occupied, so he decided to climb to the top of one of the stairways and await his scheduled rendezvous. From where he stood atop the steps, he was able to spot the Land Rover parked at the base of the hill. For a moment he considered giving Pierre a wave but decided against it. Too touristy, he concluded, and rather futile, considering the lack of light, which raised the obvious question—why hadn't they brought along a flashlight?

As the minutes passed and the music throbbed on, Adam's unease welled within. No visitor of the night had made an appearance. To think they would have come this far and ended up with a flat zero for their effort was disconcerting, to put it mildly. To make matters worse, he decided he might as well play tourist and take a quick look inside at the skeletal remains of the building. Fortunately, there was enough of the ambient light to probe the interior without bumping his head against one of the stone walls. As he peeked into one enclosure after the other, he murmured, "This could have been the servants' quarters...or this could have been the kitchen...or this could have been the library..."

Adam had just withdrawn his head from one room when all of a sudden, the background music, which had been building to a crescendo, abruptly stopped, bringing a deafening silence to the scene. Immediately, a vision of people collapsing to the ground in voodoo reverie came to mind. "Enough of this dallying," he whispered to himself. He turned to leave, only to discover his pathway out was blocked by the shadowy figure of a man who stood no more than ten feet from him. Small in stature, the guy bore a smile that stretched from ear to ear across a chalk-like painted face. Unfortunately, the knife he held at his side belied his cheerful countenance. He must have skipped out on the party early to carry out his assignment, Adam reckoned. That means he still has the evil spirit in him. Without a doubt, the message from the anonymous sender he had traveled all this way for was about to be delivered. For a guy who recoiled at the sight of a needle, Adam was unnerved at the thought of a shiv slicing into him.

The smile never left the goon's face as he lunged at Adam, swiping at him across the chest. The thrust drew first blood, but Adam was not about to let him score a second. In attempting another strike, the assailant tripped on a protruding rock and was momentarily thrown off balance, giving Adam the opportunity to thrust a fist deep into the attacker's throat. The blow knocked the guy to the floor. Mr. Smiley attempted to scramble to his feet to resume the assault. Adam, however, grabbed him by the wrist and swung him hard against the stone wall, simultaneously separating him from the knife, wiping the smile off his face, and leaving a deep gash on the side of his head. The assailant at that point apparently had had enough, slowly raising his hands in a gesture of surrender before beating a hasty retreat toward the entrance way.

Adam drew a handkerchief from his pocket and with it picked up the knife. After a brief pause to collect himself, he headed out of the palace and back down the hill to the car. Nearing the gap in the fence he began to feel a little woozy and strangely cold and wet. He stumbled over a clump of turf, barely managing to keep his feet on the ground.

"Adam! What the hell happened?" he could hear Pierre call out, as his compatriot rushed toward him. "You're bleeding bad, buddy."

"I got the message," was all he could say.

———

Pierre rushed the Land Rover back into Milot, at one point pulling to the side of the road to call out to a pedestrian. "Can you help us, please? We need to see a doctor right now."

The passerby shrugged his shoulders, as if he didn't understand, so Pierre went vernacular. "*Eske ou ka ede nou, souple? Nou bezwen yon dokte touswit.*"

The man promptly launched into a series of hand signals,

interspersed with phrases foreign to Adam. "*Ou konprann,*" he said when finished.

"I understand," Pierre said. "*Mesi!*"

He turned to Adam. "There's a hospital four blocks down and a half-mile to the left," he said. "You okay?"

"I'll live."

The hospital, it turned out, was not a fully functional hospital at all, but a neighborhood medical facility, similar in appearance to a small army field hospital. It was comprised mainly of two medium-sized tents surrounded by several smaller ones. "I'm guessing it's a temporary operation, placed here to relieve the demand on the main hospital," Pierre speculated on their arrival. "Could be the main one is undergoing an expansion or renovation."

Adam ended up in one of the larger tents, which served as an emergency room. Shortly, the doctor on duty, a woman by the name of Dr. Damaur, according to her badge, was at his side, examining his wound. A comely woman with carbon-black eyes and a light chocolate complexion, she had a voice as soft as cashmere. "You've lost a significant amount of blood," she said, following a brief exam, "but not enough to require a transfusion. We will give you a sedative...then clean, close, and bandage the wound. As a precaution we'll keep you overnight in the recovery tent. You should be out of here first thing in the morning."

"Okay, I'm in love," Pierre said from his bedside chair upon her departure. "What do I do now?"

"You can go bash your head against a wall and hope she's still on duty when you return—that is, if you can stumble your way back. By the way, what do you plan on doing while I'm being worked on?"

"I'm going to go out and buy you a new change of clothes. Of course, I'll put it on my expense account."

"And then what?"

"Sleep in the car. Beats sitting in a chair all night."

A nurse arrived with the sedative and in short order Adam lapsed into a deep sleep. When he awoke, he was in the recovery room...or recovery tent to be precise. His body rhythm told him it was early morning. A large bandage covered his wound and from all outward appearances the procedure went fine. It took twenty-five stitches to close it, the nurse informed him, his soreness vouching for the knife's lengthy swipe across his chest. The tent he was in housed close to a dozen cots, all of them filled. One at the far end of the enclosure, in particular, grabbed his attention. It was occupied by a man with a thick bandage wrapped around his head and a wide smile nailed to his face, a smile easily recognizable and aimed directly at him. To his credit the guy did manage to remove the paint from his face. Or maybe the medical staff did. It was probably not all that unusual for a voodoo party reveler to end up needing medical help. It all made sense, considering this was no doubt the closest facility in the area where the guy could get emergency treatment. Presently, they were like two rival animals at a watering hole, wary of each other, yet holding to a temporary truce. It was a good thing the guy was transferred to the room during the dark of night, Adam mused, or else he may have been tempted to finish the job he had been handed. By whom was the question yet to be determined.

Pierre arrived at his side at nearly the same time as Dr. Damaur, who was making her morning rounds. Probably a coincidence, but Adam couldn't help but wonder if his companion had been peeking around the corner to see if she was on duty before he made his appearance. "Nice timing," he whispered to him.

"How are you feeling?" the doctor asked, checking his wound.

"Very well," he replied, hoping to hurry his release. "How long before the stitches can be removed?"

"One to two weeks."

"I plan on being home by then, doctor."

"Removing stitches is a simple procedure. I'm sure your doctor back home will gladly accommodate you," she replied, glancing at her clipboard. "There is one matter to attend to before you leave, however. We are required to notify the local police of wounds that are obviously the result of an assault. An officer is scheduled to stop by shortly to question you about the incident."

"What makes you think it was an assault?" Adam asked.

Her answer came in the form of a knowing smile that slowly crossed her engaging face. "The extent of the wound and what caused it tells the tale."

"What about the fellow down the way with the bandaged head. What's the story on him?" he dared to ask. "Is the cop going to talk to him?"

"A patient's medical information is confidential, as I'm sure you know," she responded, without even a glance at the patient he was referring to. "Let's just say there are some people who will trip over their own feet rushing down some steps and end up bashing their head," she added, repeating the fake story she no doubt heard from Mr. Smiley.

"I see," Adam said, at which point the doctor gracefully stepped away to continue her rounds.

"Yep, she can stitch me up anytime," Pierre said, before turning his attention back to Adam. "Last night you said a message was delivered by your attacker. What was the message?"

"Stop doing what you're doing."

"Meaning stop with the searching."

"You got it."

"I have some overnight news for you."

"Oh, yeah?"

"Do you want to take a guess on who's camped out in a back corner of the parking lot out front?"

"In a blue Chevy, I suppose."

"Adam, I don't care if he is trained in surveillance methods; there was no way he was tailing us on our trip up, unless he was hanging twenty miles behind. The question is how did he know we were here?"

"I don't want you to look now but the guy with the bandaged head I was mentioning to the doctor, the guy occupying the last cot at the far end of the opposite side of the room. He's the one who cut me."

"Oh, yeah?" Pierre said, doing his best to keep his eyes from straying to the man Adam was referencing.

"To answer your question, he knows we're here. No doubt he informed his enabler of the incident who in turn informed Flint."

"Do you want to confront Flint...see what his game is?"

"I think we know what his game is. Our game now is to beat him at his, so we can get on with our mission. Otherwise, we might be leading him and his cohorts directly to our target, that is, if we locate him first."

"So what are you going to tell this local cop when he stops by for his little chat?"

"I'm still mulling that over, my friend. In the meantime, here's what I'd like for you to do. Go over to the wounded one and introduce yourself to him as my personal ambassador. Tell him at any moment a cop is scheduled to drop by to interview me as part of an investigation into my case. Tell him in return for my not identifying him as my attacker—and remind him we have the knife with his fingerprints on it —I will expect him to provide you with the name of the person who gave him the order to hunt us down. Okay?"

"Sure…my pleasure."

Pierre nonchalantly strolled down the hallway toward Mr. Smiley, stopping a few paces from his cot to look back at Adam and jab his thumb in the direction of where he was headed to verify it was indeed the right man he was about to confront. Adam nodded yes and as if on cue, a uniformed man of large stature, wearing a white shirt, dark blue pants, and light blue cap entered the enclosure. The man paused to first glance around the room and then at a note he was carrying, before heading in Adam's direction. The guy wore blue shoulder patches with two yellow stripes on each, indicating he was of low rank, much in keeping with the slovenly appearance he had on display. Reaching Adam's side, he introduced himself and explained the reason for his presence. The interview turned out to be a rote exercise for the most part, the officer assuming an at ease stance while in passable English reciting from a clipboard a list of questions regarding the sequence of events leading up to the attack. In response Adam could not have been more vague with each of his answers, wrapping them in plenty of uncertainty. Never in the course of the questioning did he reveal he had a traveling companion with him, mentioning only that there were no witnesses to the actual assault. Occasionally, he would glance past the officer to check on Pierre and his assailant who he was glad to see no longer had a smile plastered on his face. At the close of the interview, the officer handed him a pamphlet listing resources available should he need assistance. He also handed him a contact card in case he wanted to get in touch with authorities. With that, he turned to exit the room, but not before Adam stopped him in his tracks with a question. "Say, officer, you never did ask for a description of the assailant."

The officer scanned the notes on his clipboard and nodded affirmatively. "You know, you're right. Maybe it was because you said there were no witnesses," he said, attempting to cover his embarrassing omission.

"I was a witness," Adam replied emphatically.

"Good. You got a description...give me a description," he said, putting pen to paper.

Adam looked down the hallway toward his bandaged assailant chatting with Pierre. "Yeah, I can give you one. He's a white guy of middle age and medium build...an American, I'm sure...with a haircut that looks like it belongs on a Franciscan monk. And here's a bit of inside information, officer, as to his whereabouts. At this moment he's sitting in a blue Chevy automobile parked in the back corner of the parking lot out front."

The officer looked up from his clipboard in surprise. "How do you know this?"

"I asked to get a breath of fresh air a short while ago and a kind nurse wheeled me out front for a few minutes. It was then I spotted him. He should still be there. He must have followed me here. I think he may be waiting to get a second go at me for whatever reason."

"Okay, we'll make sure that doesn't happen."

"And officer...I'm not going to press charges. I don't want to create an international incident. However, I will if he continues to threaten me. I suggest you get him out of here. As an American, I feel he is a disgrace to our country and should be kicked out of yours before he goes preying on other innocent tourists. It doesn't look good for either of our countries."

"I agree...I'll get him on his way. If he complains, I will take him in for questioning," he said.

"By the way, what did you say your name was?"

"Antoine Barbet."

"Thank you, Antoine. I'll be sure to pass on to the Haitian authorities your exemplary conduct in this matter."

Looking pleased, the officer bowed his head and turned to leave.

Seeing him headed out the building, Pierre ambled back to Adam's side.

"How'd it go?"

"As well as could be expected. How'd it go on your end?"

Pierre pulled from his pocket a crumpled slip of paper and handed it to Adam. On it he had scribbled a name...Vincent Perone...the doctor who had signed Coulter's death certificate, Adam recalled. "No surprise there," Adam said, "more a confirmation."

"What next?"

"Next is getting out of here, which I'm told I can do as soon as I sign the discharge papers."

———

Exiting the facility Pierre stopped to look around. "I don't see Flint's car."

"He probably had some more pressing business to take care of," Adam said.

"More pressing business than our business?" Pierre asked, dumbfounded.

"Manufactured business," Adam said. "I'll explain later."

They were deliberating their next move when they passed an open-air tent that had been set up on grounds adjacent to the parking area. At first glance it appeared to be some sort of hospitality tent. Large wicker baskets filled to the brim with fruits and vegetables were aligned atop an elongated wooden table. Several people were milling about, checking the offerings, including Dr. Damaur. "I say we stock up on some supplies to take on the road with us, don't you agree?" Pierre asked, eyeing her presence.

"Sure," Adam said, unwilling to deny his friend a final engagement with the love of his life.

"You gentlemen in the mood for some healthy snacks?" she asked upon their approach.

"Are you in charge of this operation?" Pierre asked.

"I am at the moment. We take our turns. It's something we offer as a treat to patients and visitors alike."

"Free of charge?"

"Free of charge."

"The question is how do you find the time, doctor?" Adam asked, fingering a ripe apple he had snatched from a basket.

"It's a volunteer operation. Everyone on the staff lends a hand. This is my hour to lend one."

"Who provides the produce?" Pierre asked.

"Caring farmers as well as caring individuals. A good portion of it comes courtesy of my own brother."

"He's a farmer?" Adam asked, casually tossing the apple he had in hand back into the basket.

"No, he's a priest. He and a helpful assistant of his maintain a sizable garden on the parish grounds. Incidentally, you may be interested in knowing his helper is a countryman of yours...a very talented fellow for sure."

Adam immediately locked eyes with Pierre before asking his next question. "By chance, is this helper of his a white American?"

"Yes, he is. Why do you ask?"

Adam retrieved the photo of David Coulter from his pocket and displayed it to the doctor. "Is this the fellow?"

Dr. Damaur took one look. "That's him," she said, a dose of curiosity in her voice. "Is he a friend of yours?"

"No," Adam responded. "A relative of his asked us to keep an eye out for him in case we crossed paths."

"He's not wanted by the law, is he?" she asked with a touch of concern.

"Oh no," Adam said, squashing any idea she might have of contacting her brother regarding the matter.

"Where is your brother's parish located?' Pierre asked innocently.

"In Saint-Raphael. It's only about twenty miles south of here."

Pierre looked at Adam and shrugged his shoulders as if indifferent to what he was about to propose. "It's on the way home. We might as well stop and take a look at his garden. It must be a work of art. What's the name of the parish?" he asked the doctor.

"St. Joseph's. If you like, I could draw you a map showing you the exact location."

"That would be great," Adam said.

She pulled a pen and notepad from her handbag and scribbled down the directions for them. "Don't forget to take along some of these fruits and vegetables," she said, "and be sure to say hello to my brother for me. His name is Father Jude."

"Will do," Pierre said.

She handed each a paper bag with which to stash the produce. When finished, the two were effusive in expressing their appreciation. "Safe travels," she said in return.

"I'd say this medical stay was a good idea," Pierre cracked on the way to the car. "Who would have known that slice across the chest you took would end up pointing us in the right direction?"

"What's the old adage…no pain, no gain," Adam said, feeling a tinge of it as he loaded his bag of goodies into the back seat of the car. "Now, let's get the hell out of here before someone manages to catch up with us."

CHAPTER EIGHT

The search for the location of Overseas Missions United turned out to be a bit more complicated than Tamra had originally expected. A check of the phone book, directory assistance, real estate records, local church organizations, medical associations, and pertinent government agencies turned up nothing. Momentarily stumped, she decided to make a quick trip to the downtown library to research the annual city directory entries, one of the most overlooked resources in tracking an organization's location, she had learned from past experience. Similar to a phone book, the city directory furnished much more information, including lists of officers. Compiled by a private enterprise via a mailed survey, it frequently incorporated listings not found in other standard directories.

With the latest volume in hand, Tamra promptly found a listing for the OMU organization in the alphabetical section. It was shown to be located in a commercial enterprise called the Metro Executive Center located in central Tampa. Why it was listed in a city directory while not appearing in the other standard resources she had checked could be easily explained. It had to do with the compilation method employed by the publisher, which involved sending out survey forms directly to all businesses located in the region. Whereas most businesses would fill out the form for promotional purposes, there were those who wished to keep a low profile for whatever reason, nefarious or not. Or, they simply would fail to submit it. Tamra's guess was that OMU didn't submit it. So, how did it end up in the directory? Most commercial centers of significant size contain a management office. This office invariably receives a survey itself and in its response often will list all of the tenants over whom it presides. Such was the case in this instance, she surmised.

She jotted down the address and unit number for the organization, as well as the name of the sole member of management listed—John Warnick—the fellow Adam had alerted her to. She also made note of the phone number but decided to forego a call in favor of a personal visit.

———

The Metro Executive Center was a rectangular, two-story, terracotta-hued edifice of considerably larger size than Tamra anticipated and nicely decorated, she discovered. The structure's centerpiece was an interior atrium furnished with widely spaced clusters of bamboo tables and chairs, surrounded by large potted plants comprised mainly of ficus trees. A signboard listing the building's tenants was located approximate to the main entrance. On it were listed the names of real estate agents, financial advisers, independent insurance firms, accountants, and the like. A post office station and a coffee shop were also included.

Tracing the listings, she discovered OMU was located on a second floor end unit. She climbed the stairs and began the march down an elevated walkway leading to the suite, which she soon discovered was more of a corner cubbyhole than a suite. Stenciled on the entrance door in semicircle fashion was Overseas Missions United. So compact was the unit's outward appearance that she felt hesitant to knock for fear of invading someone's private space, an inhibition she quickly dismissed. She pushed open the door and straightaway found herself facing a reception counter behind which sat a "cast member trying to look like a secretary," as Adam was inclined to say when operating in similar suspicious circumstances.

"Can I help you?" the cast member asked, tossing aside a fan magazine she had been leafing through.

"Yes, I would like to speak to John Warnick, please."

"Your name?"

"Tamra Fugit."

"Do you have an appointment?"

"No."

The woman rose from her desk and eyeballed her for an instant, as if to say this might be someone Warnick might like to see, no matter what her business was. She then turned and strode a few feet back to a partitioned off area, stuck her head inside and whispered something to the person inside. She nodded on hearing the reply and returned to the reception counter.

"Dr. Warnick would be pleased to meet with you," she said, opening a counter gate to let Tamra pass through.

Doctor? Tamra asked of herself.

"Please, have a seat Ms. Fugit," Warnick said upon her entrance.

Facing her was a middle-aged man with steely features—narrow, dark gray eyes, pointed nose, and pronounced cheekbones. His most prominent feature was a widow's peak comprised of thinning black hair slicked to the back. Altogether, an attractive guy, if not for the guileful eyes, she concluded. "What can I do for you?" he asked her in a pleasant voice.

"I saw your business listed on the signboard downstairs and thought I would check to see if your name implies what I think it does."

"And what might that be?"

"When I hear or see the term 'overseas missions,' I immediately think of overseas aid efforts, like those to poor nations. Am I close?"

Warnick leaned back in his swivel chair and rested an ankle atop the opposite knee. "You're very close. To put it in simple terms, we act as sort of a matchmaker between aid organizations and benevolently inclined individuals, perhaps like yourself, who may be interested in helping out impoverished nations in some capacity. Mainly, they are people who have no direct link to churches or other charitable organizations who could provide them access. Instead, they come to us."

"I see," she said.

"Interested?"

"Are special skills required?"

"There is a wide range of skills that are in demand, depending on the organization we partner with. Of course, medical skills are at the top of the list." Warnick pulled out a desk drawer and retrieved a printed document. "Here is an application form you can either fill out here or take with you. There's a section asking you to list every pertinent skill you've got. Once we receive the completed application, we match it up to participating organizations' needs. It is then up to them to decide if they wish to call you in for an interview."

"How long does the process take?"

"Depends on the demand for your skills."

Tamra wanted to ask what their cut was from the matchmaking but didn't, figuring this was not the appropriate time to be opening a potential can of worms. "Great…I'll take it home, fill it out, and see what happens," she said, rising from her chair. "Thank you for your time."

"How long have you lived here?" he asked, halting her movement.

She slowly retook her seat. "I've lived here for most of my life."

"So, do you have family here?" he asked.

"No…no family here," she said, drawing a look of satisfaction from him.

"A single lady with an altruistic mind. I like it."

She again rose from her chair, aware of where this conversation was headed. She could hang around a few more minutes with him, apply her feminine wiles, wait for the invitation to lunch or dinner she was confident was coming, and play it from there. That is, if the memory of a similar tactic gone astray had not popped into her head. At the time, she was new on the job, working for a boss who was himself relatively new to the profession. The case before them involved a suspected killer cop who was known as a womanizer. At Adam's request—not his demand, mind you—she agreed to be the bait to lure the suspect into divulging critical information to the case. All it took was a night out at a favorite cop hangout, a clinging dress, a few eye contacts across a crowded bar, an introduction, several drinks, and the ruse was on, which ultimately led to the suspect's arrest and conviction. It was not without great danger and emotional cost, however, so much so Adam issued an apology to her, admitting the assignment fell outside her job description and vowing it would not be repeated. Still, in this instance there was an obvious opening she passed up. Perhaps she could have garnered additional information on OMU...connected more dots... here and in Haiti. The greater the amount of pertinent information on hand, the greater the chance for a break in the case, so the old bromide went. Yet, the rate of risk rises in proportion to the nearness of the truth, Adam would often point out to her, more so when you're flying solo and blind to the dangers lurking in your path. No, for now she would settle for what she got, which wasn't much other than she had placed a face, plain as it was, on the enigmatic Overseas Missions United.

"Thank you for your interest," Warnick said, extending his hand for a goodbye handshake.

She took it. "Thank you."

She turned to leave his office, her departure delayed once more by a final question from him. "By the way, how did you come across my name?"

How dumb can you be not to have anticipated that question! "You know...I don't recall offhand," she said, glancing at the ceiling, as if giving it some thought. "It must have cropped up somewhere during my research on overseas aid work."

Warnick nodded and on that note, she resumed her leave-taking.

———

Tamra sat in her car in the Metro Executive Center parking lot, mulling over her visit with Warnick. His asking where she came up with his name obviously caught her off guard. Yes, it was definitely something she should have been prepared to answer. She could have referenced the city directory but that would have undercut her story of just now learning of OMU from their listing on the first floor signboard. Oh well, perhaps she was making too big a thing of it. Also playing on her mind was the secretary referring to him as a doctor. Adam had mentioned in his call to her a physician by the name of Perone, but made no reference to Warnick as a doctor. When she got back to the office, she would shift her focus from OMU to Warnick in particular, but first she would sit still for a while in the hope Warnick might soon exit the building and drive off to who knows where. A little surveillance might offer an insight to his daily business, not to mention a clue to its legitimacy.

Tamra moved her car to a different spot in the parking lot next to a palm tree, which afforded her both a measure of privacy and a good vantage point. The first thing she observed from her vehicle's front seat was Warnick's secretary entering the building. She had noticed when she was leaving the office that his assistant was nowhere to be seen. Perhaps she had taken a break or run an errand. A half hour later, she spotted Warnick leaving the building. She had parked a safe distance back, but as he began to stride in her direction, a sense of unease quickly rose within her. She was about to start up her car and casually drive off when he suddenly stopped alongside a blue BMW, unlocked it, and slid inside.

She followed him out of the parking lot and down a main thoroughfare for four blocks, whereupon he pulled into a strip shopping center, coming to a stop in front of a fitness center.

From a distance Tamra eased her Jeep to a stop and watched him snatch a satchel out of his back seat and head for the gym. So, he's taking part of his lunch break to get in some exercise, she concluded. She decided to wait, figuring it would not be a long one if he was squeezing a workout into his lunch period. In the meantime, she pondered what was next for her. For certain, she needed to check out the reference to his being a doctor. She also must touch base with Adam in Haiti to fill him in on developments. Lastly, she had a late afternoon tennis match with Madison Davis on tap. How much she would like to best him on the court was lurking in the back of her mind.

She had guessed right about Warnick hurrying his workout. A half hour after he had entered the gym, he was exiting it with satchel in hand, heading for his car. She turned on her ignition the moment he edged from his parking slot and followed him out, expecting him to return to his office. But he didn't. Instead, he took a turn in the opposite direction. Again, she trailed him from a safe distance down the boulevard until he made a turn onto a side street. Soon, they were navigating an upper middle class neighborhood, marked by courtly homes and stately trees. At last, Warnick slowed his vehicle, pulling it alongside a curb in front of one of the homes.

From a half block behind, Tamra followed suit, guiding her jeep to a stop aside the curb. She watched as he stepped briskly up the walkway to the front entrance and knocked on the door. An instant later, a woman appeared to invite him inside. Tamra was too distant to gain a good look at the woman, other than she appeared middle aged. Finding herself once more facing a surveillance question of whether to linger or leave, she this time decided to head back to the office. In as unobtrusive manner as possible, she steered her vehicle past the target home, making a mental note of the address number on the mailbox. At the end of the block, she slowed her Jeep momentarily to also make note of the street name...Cricket Lane. She repeated it several times before asking herself the question: *Where have I seen or heard that name before?* Upon her return to the office, she immediately took to her computer to see what she could turn up on Warnick. It didn't take her long to come up with a four-year old entry that had appeared in a journal called the Florida Health Wire.

Tampa doctor's license suspended—
The Florida Department of Health suspended Dr. John Warnick's license to practice medicine, following a lengthy investigation. It was determined Warnick, a general practitioner, inappropriately prescribed and dispensed drugs to several of his patients over a six-month period.

In a subsequent search, she could find nothing indicating Warnick was back in the department's good graces.

Tamra bandied about in her head what she had learned. Warnick was a doctor who sometime back had fallen from grace...who was presently part of a shady organization called Overseas Missions United...who knew someone who lived on Cricket Lane. What to make of it? She drummed her fingers on her desk and then it hit her. *Of course!* She quickly brought up the file on the Coulter case to scan it. Carolina Coulter presently lived in a condo on the far edge of town. Before then, she lived in her parents' home, located on Cricket Lane. Tamra checked the numbered address she had noted while on surveillance against the address on the computer record. They were one and the same. The woman Warnick was visiting was Betty Coulter— Carolina's mother. *Well…well, it appears the fallen doctor is the new beau in Betty Coulter's life.*

It was time to call Adam and update him, she decided. She dialed his hotel room in Haiti but there was no answer. She next contacted the front desk and was told nobody on the staff had seen him or his companion since yesterday morning. "Have they checked out?" she asked.

"No," the clerk replied.

She pondered the situation. Over recent months Adam had been giving her increased decision-making authority regarding active cases during his absence. This was one of those instances she would exercise it. A year ago, she and Adam attended a public seminar titled "What We Do," sponsored by the local office of the FBI. Essentially, it delineated the types of cases the agency would take on. Tamra was convinced the OMU operation was one that would fall under the FBI's umbrella, especially the financial fraud angle. The man who had conducted the seminar was Jim Alexander, a guy Adam knew from past seminars. She checked her contacts list for his number and dialed him. A secretary answered and informed her he would be with her in a moment.

"Jim Alexander," the throaty voice announced.

"Mr. Alexander, this is Tamra Fugit from the office of Adam Fraley Private Investigations. Perhaps you remember me from your last seminar. Adam and I both attended it and met you afterward."

"Sure do…how is Adam?"

"Fine, as far as I know. Right now, he's in Haiti working on a case."

"What can I do for you, Tamra?"

She explained the entire matter relating to Overseas Missions

United. "My opinion, Mr. Alexander, is that they are operating as some sort of front for an international insurance fraud scheme...something to do with falsifying death certificates for illegal profit."

"I don't believe we have anything specifically on an outfit called Overseas Missions United, Tamra, but I can tell you what you have described is one of the oldest schemes in the fraud business. Haiti is just another one of those impoverished nations where insurance fraudsters go to die, so to speak. Here's how it goes...beneficiaries of lucrative life insurance policies produce phony death certificates that claim the insured person died in a foreign country, usually in nations dealing with a lot of chaos where document verification is sorely lacking. Some of these characters even come up with photos of funerals and bodies to buttress their claim."

"And if it works, the beneficiary and the supposedly dead person walk off with the money," she said.

"You got it. The outfit you're citing no doubt provides the perpetrators the means and the cover to pull off the scam. Of course, they get a nice kickback in return."

"The two names I mentioned...John Warnick and Vincent Perone...do they ring a bell with you?"

"Warnick...no, though I'd have to do some checking on that end. On the other hand, Perone never stops ringing the alarm bells. The guy is a fraudster extraordinaire. He can pass himself off as anybody... anywhere...anytime. He's very intelligent and extremely dangerous. He's not only a jack of all trades at white collar crime but a common street thug as well. He combines the worst traits of the two. He has had several assault charges leveled against him, including an attempted murder allegation. In fact, there's a warrant out for his arrest at this very moment. You said you met with Warnick. Did you meet or see Perone?" he asked anxiously.

"No...maybe he's still in Haiti," she suggested.

"Like I said, he could be anywhere and in any guise. Let me do some checking on this and I will get back to you...probably in the morning. Unfortunately, I'm going to be tied up in meetings the rest of the day."

Following the call Tamra felt a sense of relief in bringing the FBI in on the matter. She was sure Adam would agree this case had risen above their stated mission. Meanwhile, she had a tennis date with Madison to look forward to, which begged the question...was this a date, or a sporting contest, or both?

CHAPTER NINE

Madison Davis prided himself on his relationships with female patients. Never had he crossed the line to engage in a personal relationship with any of them, which seemed to be the issue of the day both within the profession and outside it, according to media accounts. God knows, he certainly had the opportunities. Why was it that husbands, boyfriends, partners, lovers, or whomever could not grasp the fact it was not physical intimacy that was the ultimate goal of women in a relationship, but the intimacy of thought? And all they had to do to achieve it was listen! So simple an approach, but so filled with land mines for the therapist who was skilled at achieving this intimacy, while still being able to maintain a professional distance with his patients. For the unethical practitioner the next step was simple. Once he achieved intimacy of thought with the patient, he could easily convince her physical intimacy was a natural therapeutic step in the process of reaching full intimacy with the significant other in their life, and who better to demonstrate it than the therapist who understands her best? In other words, you've got to experience the totality of the process to become capable of it. As for the profession's recent crackdown on the predatory therapist problem, it seemed to have had little effect. The rules and regulations regarding a therapist's conduct may have changed, but human nature had not, nor would it ever, at least in his lifetime. That's not to say he, like other reputable therapists, couldn't take what he had learned to the outside world and apply it to a situation he deemed important to his emotional well-being. In this case, his budding relationship, if you could call it that, with Tamra Fugit.

Enough with the intimacy of thought, he mused, as he watched her gracefully stroll across the park grass in her light pink shorts and top as she made her way to join him courtside. The sight of her only increased his already consuming ardor. The woman would have to go out of her way to look bad, he ruminated, and he was not sure that would even work. "Don't think for a minute of passing on her," a buddy of his advised on hearing of his interest in her. "If she's all you say she is, you'll be kicking yourself the rest of your life for not going for it."

"Are you saying I shouldn't pass on making a pass?" came his flip reply.

"Hey, from a woman's standpoint, it boils down to who's making the pass, or advance, or move...or whatever you like to call it," his buddy went on. "And remember, the mood determines the move. I know shrinks don't like to be crass, but sometimes crassness gets you there faster than politeness. You'd better step on the gas, my friend, or you're not even going to make it to first base. From what you say, that Mr. Anonymous guy could come back into the picture at any time, leaving you empty-handed, or should I say leaving you with an empty bed. No question you need to speed the process along, something you should be able to do, given your insight into women."

There was a way to speed up the process and avoid the necessity of endless conversational foreplay, he reasoned. It had to do with the old tried-and-true human behavior modifier commonly known as the adrenalin rush.

Studies had shown a definite correlation between heightened levels of attraction and arousal following intense physical activity. How many times did Bonnie and Clyde get it on after one of their crime sprees? How lucky did the teenage boy get following a rollicking roller-coaster ride with his girlfriend? Or what about the daring suitor taking his lady friend on her first skydiving trip? The evidence is endless in supporting the fact that as the adrenaline increases, so does the level of attraction. Yes, it was time to ditch the intimacy of thought process in favor of the old adrenalin rush. Tamra was a highly competitive woman, something that was readily apparent in their first match. No question a hard-fought competition against him would stir the juices…his and hers.

"You ready for a beat-down?" she said, unsheathing her racket.

Exactly what he wanted to hear. She was joshing, of course, but not entirely.

"I don't expect this to go three sets," he countered, returning her coy smile in kind.

The match itself was all he could have asked for, a grinding affair with long rallies that took them to places on the court they otherwise would never have gone to, if executed in a less intense atmosphere. Her competitiveness continually came to the fore with every exchange…the little fist pumps after every winning point…the dejection on her face with every errant shot…the beads of perspiration glistening on her face, shoulders, and arms that slowly trickled down to even sweeter spots. Talk about wanting to be a fly on the wall in a clandestine meeting of great interest…how about wanting to be one of those bawdy beads going about their prurient way.

True to his design, if not his prediction, the match did go three sets. Yeah, it was all he could have hoped for, though the ending was not what he expected. He had played it too close in the belief he could end it at any time with a flurry of points. However, she was the one who ended it in a tiebreaker set, delivering a perfect drop shot over the net that left him standing at the baseline with a bemused look on his face.

"I don't know how I managed to come up with that last stroke," she said breathlessly, as they sat side by side on a courtside bench. She was flushed with victory. The rush of adrenaline obviously had kicked in, just as it had with him, satiating the body with a euphoria that screamed to be shared. The sight of a shapely leg only enhanced the feeling. What's more, the rush had added a luster to her skin, further evidence his prognosis was correct.

"Thanks for the workout, Tamra," he said, as he casually rested an opened hand above her knee…actually, on the inner thigh, to be precise. As expected, the flesh was firm, warm, and moist, sending an added jolt of adrenaline through him. The words to follow, however, were bitter cold and dry.

"Madison, what are you doing?" So cold were they, his hand became frozen in place. Not for long, however, for she at once snatched it with her forefinger and thumb and removed it from its resting place, as she would a piece of lint from one of her finer dresses. "Thank you for the game," she said smartly, before grabbing her satchel and sauntering away.

Madison sat there, the adrenaline completely drained from his body. What to say to his buddy, the so-called expert who urged him to speed up the process so he could at least make it to first base with her? He snickered at the thought. First base? Hell, he couldn't even make it out of the batter's box. He gazed at the palm of his hand. And they say baseball, football, tennis—whatever—are games of inches, he ruminated. The truth is you can throw the game of love into the mix. All he had to do was rest this hand of his one or two inches closer to the knee and he would have been rounding first base and on his way to second.

He positioned his hand above his knee approximate to where he placed it on Tamra's. Yeah, he was two or three inches off, alright. And here he thought he knew everything there was to know about laying a hand on a woman. Oh well, it was worth the try. In parlance foreign to his profession, he was able to cop a feel, after all, though he would need to revisit that other paper he wrote on interpersonal relationships and gender boundaries before making any further attempts.

———

"Has you father called?"

"No," Noelle replied. "He'd better make it back in time for our night out is all I've got to say."

"Don't worry. Everything will turn out fine. I bet Bobby isn't worried."

They were in Tamra's kitchen, preparing dinner, an easy one... grilled chicken and fried rice.

"Why are you crying?" Noelle asked straightaway.

"What makes you think I'm crying? By the way, did you get your homework done?" she quickly asked, pivoting the conversation.

"Yes, it's all done. Aren't you worried Daddy hasn't called?"

"He'll call, honey. He's probably very busy right now."

She was worried, not about their upcoming night out with Bobby, but Adam's failure to call. It was unlike him to not keep her abreast of his progress on a case or check on how his daughter was doing. Not like him at all.

CHAPTER TEN

JOHN WARNICK SNATCHED HIS NAMEPLATE FROM HIS DESK AND tossed it into a nearby trash can. He next got busy with the disposal of documents, grabbing and feeding fistfuls of them through an office shredder. Yeah, it was fun while it lasted, not to mention lucrative… their overseas missions scam. Now it was time to fold up shop…and fast.

"You look like you're in a hurry," the familiar voice said from behind him, setting off a warning bell in Warnick's head.

"What brings you back here?" he asked his visitor, as he continued his feeding of the shredder.

"Unfinished business."

"Our business is finished in case you hadn't heard," he dared to reply.

"All because of your stupidity," the visitor replied in a cutting voice. "You couldn't keep your hands off that Coulter woman, could you? And don't tell me it was all for love. What exactly did she do to capture your attention—waltz in here one day to check whether her missing husband might have made use of our overseas connections for his getaway and you took it from there?"

"She represented a pile of insurance money, Perone. Isn't that what Overseas Missions United was all about? It was all slated to go into the profit pool, which meant you would be getting your share down the road."

"Why do I seriously doubt that? Why do I think you were going to game the system for yourself...you know...get something on the side in addition to a little sex? Yeah, I get you the phony death certificate and you take it from there, nabbing a potential wife and nice inheritance to look forward to. And why should I believe you were planning on sharing some of that inheritance with your fellow employees—like me for instance? It's not like you were going to get rid of her anytime soon. Or were you planning on calling on me to speed up her demise?"

"You've done okay yourself with this operation," he responded. "You have no reason to complain."

His strategy in dealing with Perone in person was the same as that of everyone else in the organization. Avoid eye contact with him, if at all possible. All it took to trigger the guy was a disapproving glance at the wrong moment.

"Where's that worthless secretary of yours...spilling her guts to the FBI after tipping them off?" he asked.

"On the contrary, it was she who tipped us off."

"Tipped us off to what? The FBI getting involved?"

"No, the private investigator I told you about...the guy snooping around in Haiti. She was the one who tipped me off to him."

"Fraley? He's being taken care of."

"By who?"

"My people."

"You sure? He's there and you're here, and you know how communications are between here and there...not exactly timely or accurate."

"I have confidence in my hires, Warnick. I have no confidence in yours, like that P.I. you picked out of the yellow pages to track down Fraley. What's he done other than fart around that hellhole of a country like a chicken with its head cut off?"

"Like I said, communications are slow between here and there. Give him time."

"To do what? I told you Fraley's being taken care of and you're now telling me the operation is all over. No, I'm much more concerned with the mismanagement here on the home front that led to the law closing in. Safe to say it was due to your stupidity in taking up with that Coulter woman in the first place."

Perone paused for a reaction but none was forthcoming. "Oh yeah, your little fling started the ball rolling, leading Fraley to stick his nose into our business," he declared. "By the way, for the record, how did you get wind of his involvement?"

"There was a gal who paid us an unannounced visit here a while back who was asking suspicious questions. That worthless secretary, as you call her, made a point of getting her license plate number. It turned out our suspicions were correct. She worked for Fraley. That's when I contacted you about his involvement."

"The gal's name?"

"Tamra...or Tamara...something like that. I forget the last name."

"Must have been a looker. Rumor has it your secretary would only funnel the fetching ones your way, at your request, of course."

Warnick was tempted to stand up and confront his inquisitor. His patience had run out. Not that he had much to begin with for bullies like Perone. The problem was the guy was much more than a bully. He was a bully who could take a punch in the mouth and keep coming at you. As long as he was in Haiti, he was tolerable. Here...not so much. Still, discretion told him to keep doing what he was doing and ignore the guy as best he could in the hope he might leave. "This operation is over, Perone," he said with as much finality as he could muster. "I suggest you take care of any unfinished business you might have here and hightail it back to Haiti where your people can look out for you."

An unsettling silence between the two ensued, as Warnick deliberately turned his full attention back to his shredding operation, all the while feeling Perone's disturbing eyes boring into his back.

"Yeah, I've got some unfinished business to take care of," Perone said in his best menacing voice.

For a few moments the unsettling silence returned, until Warnick finally heard Perone's footsteps receding toward the door, leaving him wondering what or whose business Perone was going to take care of. "Why should I care, as long as it's not mine?" he asked himself, exhaling a deep sigh of relief.

CHAPTER ELEVEN

THE ROAD TO SAINT-RAPHAEL WAS A TREACHEROUS ONE, MADE SO by a sudden late-morning squall that had swept in off the northern coast. They had traveled not more than ten miles before the torrential rains transformed the route into a muddy quagmire.

"I've driven on snow, ice, and through deep sand but nothing like this," Pierre said as he struggled to keep their vehicle on a stable track in the thick of the onslaught. "The roads here are more like trails, which doesn't help."

The rain continued to beat relentlessly against the windows, overpowering the wipers. "Maybe we should pull off to the side and wait it out," Adam suggested. "We're in no hurry."

"Let's give it another mile…see if we can get beyond this," Pierre said, willing to soldier on.

It was a mile too far. Negotiating a curve at slow speed, the Land Rover lost traction in the muck and started a steady slide off the road and down a grassy incline.

"Hold on," Pierre said, rotating the wheel into and out of spins, until he could rotate no more. "The steering wheel's locked up on me," he said dejectedly. His efforts up to that point did manage to significantly slow their slide. Halting their descent was a large walnut tree against which the vehicle came to a forty-five-degree angle stop. They were close to sixty feet from the road on an incline of about thirty degrees. If not for the tree, they would have slid another ten feet to the bottom of a narrow gully.

"What now?" Pierre asked, shutting off the engine. The rain was falling in nearly horizontal sheets, limiting visibility to a few feet. "It was my decision to muscle on that got us here. I'll leave the next one to you."

"I think we're better off waiting for this thing to pass by," Adam said, settling back in his seat.

They didn't have long to wait. The fierce storm dispersed about as quickly as it arrived, allowing the sun's rays to partially reappear.

The two rolled down their windows and surveyed the landscape. "There was some kind of a little supply store we passed about two miles back," Pierre said. "Why don't I hoof it back there and see if we can get some help. Hell, there's no traffic, nor will there be for a while, so chances of someone stopping to give us a hand are zero."

"What are you going to do—call the rental company for road assistance? The chance for that is also zilch. At best, it would take them a day or two to get someone out here…that is, if road service is even an option."

"You're probably right, but I'm not in favor of sitting here and doing nothing."

"Why don't I do the hoofing back?" Adam volunteered.

"Because I speak the language—remember?" Pierre countered.

Adam's companion didn't bother to wait for a reply, shoving open the vehicle's door and hopping onto the soggy turf.

He watched Pierre trudge up the incline and onto the road where he stopped for a moment to look back and give him a parting wave before plodding on.

Adam settled in for the wait, occasionally exiting the car to stretch his legs. It was during one stretch a potential predicament caught his attention. The storm may have moved on, but the aftermath was far from over. At the bottom of the gully, a tiny stream of water had formed, a sure sign the runoff from the hills above had begun. As the minutes passed, the trickle turned into a brook, and then into a stream several feet deep, he surmised. How long it would take for it to turn into a torrent of rushing water was anyone's guess, if indeed it continued its rise. All he could do was stand and wait as images of a Land Rover spiraling down the gully like a whitewater raft played on his mind. Maybe he should peruse the applicable provisions of the rental agreement to pass the time, he jested to himself. Perhaps there was a flash flood provision in the fine print. Sure, right below the road assistance entry.

———

Pierre reached the supply station, a cinder-block structure with a flat sheet-metal roof. It had the shape of a single-level duplex with separate entrances. One side appeared to be the living quarters while the other half represented the store portion, as evidenced by the homemade decals lining its windows indicating the various supplies available.

Since the door to the store portion was propped open, Pierre decided to give it a try first. He reached an arm halfway in and knocked on it. Seconds later a young woman appeared at the door. She looked passed him, ostensibly to see if he was accompanied by anyone else or in possession of a vehicle.

"I'm an American," he said, at once wishing he hadn't.

"Congratulations," she said.

"Sorry…I was about to say you probably don't see many Americans traveling this road."

"Not on foot," she said through a grin.

She was an attractive woman with neck-length dark hair parted in the middle, jade green eyes, and cocoa brown skin. He guessed her to be in her mid or late twenties and of mixed European and Haitian descent. She wore an off-white blouse and a long denim skirt that reached to her high-top tennis shoes.

"My name is Pierre."

"Angeline," she said, completing the introduction. "What can I do for you?"

"A friend and I were driving down this road during the storm when our car skidded off the road and down an incline. To put it bluntly, we're stuck in the mud and in need of help."

"How far from here?"

"About a mile and a half…maybe two."

"How far down the incline?"

"Sixty feet, give or take a few. It's sitting on a pretty steep incline… up against a tree to be exact."

"So you're much closer to the bottom of the gully than the road."

"Sounds like you're very familiar with the lay of the land."

"As many times as I've driven this road, I should be familiar with every square inch of it by now…don't you think?"

"Yes ma'am."

"If you'll excuse me…" She stepped outside the door, moving him back from it. "Follow me," she said, closing the door behind them.

He followed her around to the back of the building to a gravel parking area where the sight of an old, sturdy-looking Ford pickup with a hitch ball mounted on the back instantly lifted his spirits.

She walked past the pickup to a dilapidated shed, swung open its creaky door, and began to retrieve one old carpet after another from inside, tossing them on the ground. "Can you put these in the truck bed?" she asked.

"Sure," he replied and went to work. "You know, we expect to pay you for your help," he called back to her.

"Gracious of you, except we take that as an insult in these parts when it comes to lending a hand," she said, toting to the pickup a long length of rope with a clip on each end and a small shovel. She quickly tossed them atop the carpet mats. "Hop in," she said, circling to the driver's side. Once inside Pierre noticed the vehicle had a converted floor shift. Angeline grabbed it like she was the one who had done the converting. Seconds later they were headed down the road at a slow, steady pace. The blazing sun already was beginning to bake away some of the surface water from the trail and dry the ridges of the ruts he and Adam had left in their wake.

"Let's hope your friend and your truck are still there," she said, maintaining a safe pace.

Pierre gave her a quizzical look. "Why wouldn't they be?"

She nodded toward the gully. "Haven't you noticed the runoff? It happens here quite often after a heavy downpour."

Pierre took a look out the window. "You make it sound worrisome."

"It's something to keep your eye on. It's a narrow gully so the water rises fast. Chances are it will crest before it reaches your vehicle. If not, there may be some tossing and turning of it."

"Our rental vehicle to be precise."

She smiled…an engaging one. "Where are you from in the States, Pierre?"

He liked that…hearing her say his name with that French accent. "Originally, from rural Louisiana. More recently, from Tampa, Florida."

"Is Louisiana where you learned Creole? You speak it very well."

"I mostly learned it there. I have spent some time in this country on an overseas work assignment. It gave me the chance to polish it."

"What sort of work?"

"Industrial painting. What about you…do you run that store of yours by yourself?"

"No, my father helps me. He originally built the business, but now he's getting to an age where he can only lend a helping hand. His health is failing. It won't be long before I'll be going it alone."

Pierre paused a moment in his questioning to let the reality of her situation sink in.

"So you sell food and fishing bait supplies," he continued. "How's the demand holding up?"

"It fluctuates. We're not far from Grand Riviere or the northern seacoast for that matter. Tourists and locals on their way to either of those spots often make a point of stopping to pick up supplies."

"I take it you're not a city girl, stuck out here all by your lonesome."

"First of all, I'm not stuck out here. I'm here by choice. I love the outdoors and the rural life. I love Haiti."

Approaching the bend in the road where the Land Rover left it, she slowed the vehicle. "That must be your friend ahead of us…the man off to the right leaning against the car."

"It's him alright," Pierre said, noting the rushing water had risen to within a couple of feet of the vehicle.

———

Adam spotted the pickup coming down the road with Pierre occupying the passenger seat. Not a minute too soon, he thought. The swollen creek had slowed its rise but was still inching dangerously close to the vehicle.

The pickup pulled to a stop directly above him. Pierre and a woman driver jumped from the truck and stepped gingerly down the soggy incline to where he stood.

"Adam…I'd like for you to meet Angeline," Pierre said by way of introduction.

He nodded his greeting. "So you're our rescuer."

"I'm not sure about that, but we'll see," she said in excellent English, stepping back to survey the scene. "To tow you up, I'm going to need room on the left side of the road to maneuver the pickup. As you can see, there's a hill butting up against it at the point we are now. A little farther down, the hill levels off with the road." She took another few steps back to once more examine the situation. "We can attach the rope and I can drag your vehicle along, hopefully parallel to the creek, until I reach the leveled land on the far side of the road with my truck. I will then have room to drag you up to the road. That is, if everything goes as planned," she added with what to Adam was a very captivating smile.

He looked to Pierre and shrugged his shoulders. "Sounds like a plan. Who rides with whom? Or do we even need anyone in our vehicle?"

"It might be helpful in case the rope breaks, which it shouldn't," Angeline said. "In the unlikely case it does, you may have to steer it as best you can away from the water."

"You take the wheel of our vehicle. I'll ride with Angeline," Pierre said.

Adam gave his compadre a coy look.

"I can't swim," Pierre said, smothering a smile.

"Sure you can't."

The question of who would ride with whom was settled when an old, battered flatbed truck unexpectedly came rumbling up the road, grabbing the attention of the three onlookers. Straightaway, the question was posed by the truck's surprise appearance…what if this occurred while the rope was stretched tight across the road?

"Pierre, why don't you keep an eye on the road while Adam and I handle the vehicles," Angeline suggested on the clunker's passing.

"Will do," Pierre said. "There is one other problem, however."

"What's that," she asked.

"The steering mechanism locked up on us. The vehicle can't be steered. Maybe it was a cable or belt that snapped."

"Was it shimmering before it locked?"

"Yep, shimmering and shaking. All body parts, human and mechanical, had the shakes, including the speedometer, and we were running well under the speed limit, that is if there is one around here."

"Then it likely wasn't a cable or belt," she confidently stated. "Mud can cake your wheel wells. Those were the symptoms you were experiencing. We'll need to get the mud off before it dries."

"Your four-wheel drive is locked in…right?" she asked.

"Yes, ma'am," Pierre replied.

"Try not to brake your vehicle," Angeline instructed Adam. "It will only make matters worse. You always want to maintain momentum when moving through mud this thick."

By luck, the Land Rover had tow knobs fastened to its front and rear ends. Angeline returned up the hill and proceeded to attach one end of the rope to the back of her pickup and stretch it down to the front end of the Land Rover, at which point the first glitch in the plan became glaringly clear. The tow rope was three feet short.

Angeline shook her head. "I thought I had enough."

Adam exited the vehicle and stood by Angeline's side. Soon, Pierre joined them, having observed the problem from afar. Together, the three stood there, hands on hips, contemplating the predicament and the options available to them, none of which seemed viable. For openers there was no time to return to the store for more rope. Secondly, attempting to drive or push the Land Rover by hand a few feet further up the hill was too risky. The vehicle already was precariously positioned against the tree and any movement could send it slipping into the water. The same held true for Angeline's pickup. There was no room left for her to maneuver it closer to the Land Rover without leaving the road and launching it into a downward slide. Tether the rental to the tree? Nope, not nearly enough rope to secure it.

All the while, the funnel of rushing water was inching up, lapping at the Land Rover's tires.

"Gentlemen, I'd like for you to unbuckle your belts and give them to me," Angeline abruptly said, with a soft smile on her face.

The two men glanced at each other, shrugged, and at once complied with the lady's command, unbuckling and handing over their belts. "Sturdy leather...that helps," she said, stretching them out. "Hold on, I think I have something in my glove compartment that may help." Up the hill she scrambled and moments later returned with a roll of duct tape in hand. She took the first belt, buckled it and looped it around the vehicle's front tow bar. She then took the second belt, looped it through the first and buckled it, providing her enough extra length to clip the end of the tow line to the leather strap. She then wrapped plenty of duct tape around the buckles to buttress them. "Let's hope they hold," she said when finished.

"They held our bellies in," Adam quipped.

"A stress test if there ever was one," Pierre chimed in.

Angeline hustled back up the hill to her pickup, while Adam and Pierre returned to their original positions...Adam in the driver's seat and Pierre back on the road to continue his lookout. Carefully, Angeline set the truck in motion, taking out all of the slack in the rope. Once it was taut, she pressed forward, dragging the Land Rover below along with it.

Adam sat with his feet free of the brake and his hands removed from the steering wheel. He might as well have been sitting on the passenger side, he reckoned. The Land Rover was being dragged along at nearly a thirty-degree angle. Several times its rear dipped into the edge of the swollen stream but never substantially into it, thanks to Angeline maintaining a taut rope. So far, the leather belts were holding, but for how long? Gradually, Adam felt a shift in the pull of the vehicle. He figured Angeline must have reached the leveled-off area and was making a left turn onto it. In short order, she was dragging the rental directly and steadily upward toward the road. All looked good until five feet short of the road everything abruptly came to a halt. The next thing he saw was Angeline and Pierre jogging in his direction. "I hit a dead end," she said. "This is as far as I can drag you."

"What next then?" Adam asked. "There's little chance we can advance this thing without the benefit of a tow."

"First, we have to clean the wheel wells as best we can of mud, then place the mats I brought along under your car to give you traction. That should be enough to get you to the road," she said with calm sureness. "Pierre, could you go grab the mats and shovel while I detach the rope to give your vehicle free rein? Adam, why don't you prop some of those branches that have been blown down by the storm behind your rear wheels to keep you in place."

Adam gathered some of the limbs and was propping them behind the wheels when Pierre returned with the mats and shovel. They placed the mats in front of all four wheels and had enough remaining to line them clear to the road. Meanwhile, Angeline, having detached the tow rope, grabbed the shovel and went to work removing clumps of mud from under the wheel wells, paying little heed to the mud bath she was getting.

"All this in a skirt," Adam murmured under his breath to Pierre. "Rural Haitian women stick to traditional garb," Pierre whispered back. "You won't find many of them running around in pants."

"Okay, my friend, it's all yours," Pierre said, stepping back alongside Angeline when the preparation was complete. "Remember to keep your momentum," she called out to Adam who had manned the driver's seat.

Adam ignited the engine, put the car in gear, and pressed down on the accelerator with moderate force, propelling the vehicle ahead in fits and starts. Sensing he was about to lose momentum, he pressed down harder, the mats giving him enough traction to propel the vehicle five feet up and onto the road in one fell swoop.

"Hurrah!" Pierre shouted, shooting his arms into the air in triumph.

Angeline circled her pickup back onto the road adjacent to the Land Rover. The three next gathered up all the mats along with the rope and shovel and tossed them into the back of it, but not before the two men had reclaimed their belts. As for the rental, it appeared none the worse for wear. Other than the spattering of mud, there were no dents or nicks to be seen. Furthermore, the steering mechanism appeared back to normal, thanks to the cleaning of the wheel wells.

"There's an old saying truckers have when driving in these conditions...'drive as slowly as possible and as fast as necessary,'" she advised them.

"Are you sure we don't owe you for this?" Pierre asked.

"I'm sure," she said, standing there with her arms, hair, skirt, blouse, and shoes caked with mud. She took a step back and wiped her brow with the back of her hand, leaving a streak of muck across it. Somehow, it lent an earthly charm to the woman, Adam observed. From the mirthful look on Pierre's face, he appeared to agree. "You fellows take care now," she added, before swinging open the pickup's door.

Adam stood to the side with his hands clasped behind his back. A sudden dejected look on Pierre's face led him to sense his companion wanted to say more. Better hurry, he mused, or else you're going to miss your one and only chance.

"Angeline!" Pierre called out, halting her climb into the cab. "Are you going to be home a month from today?"

She thought a moment. "I should be...why?"

"I plan on coming back to Haiti."

"For what purpose?" she asked, her hand fixed to the opened door.

"To see you."

She flashed that special smile of hers. "I'd like that," she said and climbed into the truck.

———

Pierre headed the Land Rover down the road toward Saint-Raphael. The euphoria emanating from him was equal to that of a dozen ardent suitors, Adam figured. "Well…well…well," he razzed, reaching over to nudge his friend on the shoulder. "If it isn't Mr. Smooth. Where does this leave Dr. Damaur?"

"That was make-believe, Adam. Dr. Damaur travels in a different lane than I do. Not so Angeline. She is a country girl. I swear she is the first woman to take my mind off my late wife. Don't get me wrong. I wasn't looking for someone to take her off my mind. It just happened she did. Does that make sense?"

"It makes perfect sense. I say this as the guy caught in the middle of the sparks flying between you two."

Suddenly, Pierre took one hand from the steering wheel and slapped himself upside the head. "Hell, I forgot to get her phone number!"

"Not to worry," Adam said. "Tamra can dig it up, as well as an address, in no time. Who knows? One day soon you may drop anchor here—for a very good reason, I might add."

"I learned from my previous experience that working here on a temporary basis and living here on a permanent one requires a radical change of lifestyle, Adam. You don't see Haiti topping the lists of recommended places overseas to settle down, do you?"

"Listen, all of those articles and books coming out on the market telling you where the best places to live are presumptuous, to say the least. Follow your own personal criteria, not theirs. Besides, if you've got the right woman by your side, you can live just about anywhere that's half decent."

"Nome, Alaska?" Pierre joshed.

"Damn right…especially Nome…the cuddling capital of the world, from what I hear," Adam said, nudging him once again on the shoulder.

"What do you consider the happiest time of your life, Adam?" Pierre asked, still basking in the afterglow of his good fortune with Angeline.

"That's an easy one for me…the adoption of my daughter," he quickly replied. "Otherwise, it's the childhood events—family Christmas rituals, neighborhood block parties, sandlot games with buddies. For me the best of times were those shared with other people, though an occasional nap alone on a grassy knoll on a lazy summer afternoon watching the clouds drift by wasn't too shabby of a pastime. How about you?"

"Much the same. Other than my marriage, I also go back to my childhood days—catching fireflies in a jar, fishing with my father, and all things Christmas, of course. Not to throw a downer into this, but I've always believed the happy times are linked directly to the sad ones, as if one is a precursor or a precondition for the other. In my case, a marriage followed by a wife's passing…"

"For me, the death of Noelle's mother followed by my adoption of her," Adam interjected.

"Forget about the lows. Do you suppose any of our highs in the future will match or exceed those?" Pierre asked.

"You may have a good start on one with what just happened back there," Adam suggested with a grin.

"A single memory does not make for a happy time," Pierre pointed out. "You have to string together a succession of them to meet the definition."

"Maybe so, but it sure looks like you've got a good start on one."

Their slog south continued. At one point a mini mudslide spawned by the storm blocked the road, requiring a five-mile detour over another unpaved road. By dusk they finally reached Saint-Raphael where road conditions appeared back to normal, meaning no more rapid back and forth twists of the steering wheel by Pierre to avoid ruts. Tired and hungry for something other than fruits and vegetables, they stopped at a small restaurant to gorge their stomachs with stewed chicken and wine. Whipped by the weariness of the day, they decided to call it one. They would wait till the morning to seek out St. Joseph's parish and David Coulter. The proprietor of the restaurant tipped them off to a rooming house close by where they could crash. The room, it turned out, had two cots. The house itself had a communal bathroom. For them it was the Ritz.

CHAPTER TWELVE

Tamra sat at her desk, mulling over her to-do list for the day ahead. Among other things, she needed to contact two clients whose cases had been placed on hold pending the outcome of the Coulter matter. She wanted to let them know they had not been forgotten. Amid other pressing items, Adam's whereabouts weighed heavily on her mind as did the lingering resentment from the unpleasant episode with Madison. It was not that her past experiences with men were free of such incidents. No, for whatever reason, they just seemed to be occurring at a faster pace lately. Little did she know that her experiences with the opposite sex were about to get much worse.

She had picked up the phone to dial a client regarding another case when the office door swung open and through it walked a man whose physical presence alone lowered the room temperature to freezing. The man reeked of creepiness—fleshy face, bulging eyes, thick lips, and scraggly, unkempt hair. Yet, the features did not match with the stylish gray suit he wore. It was as if some anonymous benefactor had handed him a wad of cash to go buy one for a job interview he was going on.

The visitor strode to her desk, picked up the nameplate, and noted the name engraved on it. "Tamra," he said, before returning it. "I must have the right place."

"Can I help you?" she asked in her usual polite greeting voice.

He scooted out the chair in front of her desk and helped himself to a seat. "Aren't we going to introduce ourselves first?" he asked, reaching out a hand.

She took it...a clammy one...the kind that could leave a crawl streak on your palm. "Tamra," she said.

A twisted smile crossed his face. "Vincent," he responded in a squeaky doll-like voice. "Vincent Perone, and please don't call me Vinny. Vincent is the preferred choice. It was the only thing my mother got right in her attempt at motherhood." He chuckled. "Nope... Mother's Day was no cause for celebration in our house."

The sirens in her head were all going off now.

She repeated her question. "Okay, what can I do for you, Vincent?"

"I need an investigator to track someone down for me."

"Our investigator is currently tied up with another case at the moment."

He reached over to the entrance door adjacent to Tamra's desk and switched the latch into the locked position.

"What did you do that for?" she asked, annoyed and alarmed at the same time.

"Privacy," he said in a matter-of-fact manner.

She quickly rose from her chair and circled the desk to unlock it, but she didn't make it past him. He grabbed her by the wrist with a vice-like grip and dragged her back to her chair. "Sit the hell down. Don't you know how to treat potential clients?"

He returned to his chair. "Now...where were we? Oh yes, you were telling me your investigator is tied up at the moment. Adam Fraley —right?"

"Yes," she said, deciding to limit her responses so as not to provoke him further. Walking on eggshells it would be...for now.

"My question to you is, why haven't you replaced him yet?"

"What do you mean...replace him?"

"You haven't heard from him for a while...have you?" he asked with a snarky smile.

She sat silent.

"Well…have you?"

"He's been busy with the case he's on."

"Not the kind of boss to leave you in the dark—is he? Calls whenever he can—right? Go ahead…give him another call…see if he's at least left a message for you."

Tamra hesitantly picked up the phone and dialed the motel in Haiti. The desk clerk informed her Adam and Pierre had not been seen for some time.

"Have they checked out?" she asked.

"No," came the answer. She hung up the phone and looked to her visitor who sat with a smirk on his face. He had animal eyes… something not human in them, she observed.

He chuckled again "Has he checked out? I can answer that for you. Yeah, he's checked out alright."

Oh, God, please don't make it so. Immediately, her thoughts turned to Noelle. The girl had already lost a mother. To lose a father was unthinkable. She refused to believe it.

Suddenly, the phone rang. She wasn't about to ask him for permission to answer it. Perhaps it was Adam after all.

"Adam Fraley Investigations," she announced to the caller.

"Tamra, this is Jim Alexander over at the FBI office. I wanted to tell you…"

"No, Adam is not in at the moment," she said, interrupting him.

"Tamra, is someone there with you?" the caller asked apprehensively.

"Yes, he's the jack of all trades," she said and followed with, "I'll let him know you called…goodbye."

"Gotcha," Alexander said, a split second before she hung up.

"No more is he the jack of all trades," Perone said, reaching over to grab an apple she earlier had placed on the top of her desk. From his inside pocket he took out a knife—a switchblade with the initials VP engraved in script on the side of its pearl handle. He snapped open the business end and sliced away a piece of the fruit, tossing it in his mouth and smacking his lips as he devoured it.

"That was my lunch," she said straightforwardly.

"That was your lunch? No wonder you're so trim. I don't mind saying you're one fine-looking woman. By the way, you can mark that down as sexual harassment speak, if you like. Funny, how that works. I say it and it automatically is filed as harassment. Yet, the pretty boys say the exact same thing and you're batting those sexy eyes of yours back at them."

There was a rap on the door. They looked at each other as if questioning who would make the first move, if any. At last, Perone reached back and unlatched the door, cracking it open far enough for Madison Davis to stick his head in. "Sorry to interrupt," he said, catching her visitor out of the corner of his eye. "I just wanted to give you a quick *mea culpa* for last evening. Talk to you later," he hurriedly added, before drawing back from the door.

Cringe worthy, Tamra thought, though at the moment she would take cringe over insanity.

Perone again slipped the latch into the locked position. This time he also switched off the lights, rendering a shadowy cast to the room. "There…that's better," he said. "Now tell me…who was that clown?"

"He operates a small business in this building."

"What kind of a business?"

"He's a psychologist, I believe."

"You're kidding me!" Perone gushed with glee. "Let me guess the reason for the *mea culpa*. He was trying to diddle you last evening and you slapped him down for the clown that he is. Am I close?"

She was silent in response to his conjecture. It may have been unfair to Davis, but in a flash of gallows humor, she speculated on whose side she would be on in a clash between the two.

"So, I was right," he said. "I sense you don't care for the fellow. Want me to go make him a visit? He won't be making passes at you again. You need to stay away from those shrinks. They will be analyzing every little move you make in and out of the bedroom. You're guaranteed to end up with analysis paralysis, which can put a damper on lovemaking."

"That won't be necessary," she said.

"Yeah, I've seen my share of shrinks," he continued. "Every time I went to court the damn judge would send me for a psychiatric evaluation. It wasn't long before the shrinks they were sending me to were in need of other shrinks to deal with the mental complications of trying to analyze me. I kept telling them, 'Humans are also animals. I like to think of myself as a walking reminder of that fact.' They couldn't seem to understand it was the principle upon which I based my actions with others."

"What do you want, Vincent?" she said with a stress on the first name.

"Can't resist running your mouth, can you?" he said. "Why is it women are so suffocating, especially mothers toward their sons? My old lady was a master at it. 'Here Vincent, have some more mashed potatoes,' she would say at dinner and not let up. 'No, mother, I don't want any more mashed potatoes.' 'But they're good for you...come on, have some more.' I got so fed up with it one time, I reached into the bowl of them she was waving in front of me, grabbed a big handful, and tossed the damn potatoes into her face. Man, it was great. I may have ruined the family Thanksgiving dinner, but it did a world of good for my ego."

He finished the apple, tossed the core into the waste basket, smacked his lips, and folded the blade back into the knife's handle. Carefully, he laid it on the desk. "Oh, what a wonderful world this would be if everyone behaved like ladies and gentlemen...right?" He shook his head, "Well, sorry to spoil the thought, but it's not in us... and don't let the preachers tell you otherwise."

"What brought you back from Haiti?" she asked.

"Do you really have to ask? It should be apparent to you from what I hear. Yeah, I was in Haiti, making good money in the insurance industry, until your boss started sticking his nose into our business, which, as I'm sure you've figured out by now, is what brought me back here. You also should know I'm considered an expert within the profession on death and dying, though I have to admit the slicing and dicing can get boring after a while, especially on the dead bodies."

"Playing doctor there...were you?" she asked, unable to resist the zinger.

"You bet. I'm good at playing doctor," he said, his eyes locking on hers. "Oh, how I would have liked to have been one of the boys on your neighborhood block growing up. I would have been at the front of the line trying to play doctor with you."

"You need to grow up Vinny," she said straight out. She had had her fill of the male species for the last couple of days. Especially his kind, she thought, though she had to admit he was one of a kind, if there ever was one.

He leaned in, encroaching on every inch of her space. "The Bible says, 'The tongue is a restless evil, full of deadly poison.' Did you know one of those shrinks they were sending me to was a woman whose tongue was full of evil? Well, I sliced the evil out of her, stopped her from spewing any more of her poison, just like I plan on doing with you."

"I'm not afraid of you," she said firmly, ignoring the anger in him that was fast bubbling to the surface.

"Yes, you are, or at least you should be."

Perone took his switchblade back in hand, snapped open the blade, and rose from his chair, sending a shiver through her. At the same moment there came a loud rap on the door, causing her would-be assailant to pause and slowly lower himself back into the chair. There came a second rap, prompting him to place a forefinger on his lips to warn her to keep silent. Tamra debated whether to call out, not wanting to put whomever was at the door in harm's way. A deathly silence ensued, long enough to convince her that the opportunity to escape her tormentor had passed.

Thinking the same, Perone started to slowly rise from his chair once more when a third rapping froze him in place. "FBI here...open the door, please."

Perone eased back into his chair and folded the blade back into the handle. At the same instant the door blew open—kicked in by one of three men wearing FBI jackets, including Jim Alexander.

Perone calmly laid his knife on the desk, keeping his eyes fixed on her. "You can start batting your eyes now, Tamra," he said, in a whispered voice. "The pretty boys are here."

———

By all measures she should feel fortunate—for the capture of Perone, for the exposure of Overseas Missions United as a fraud, for the timely arrival of the FBI. Nonetheless, one measure was still outstanding—the whereabouts of Adam.

"If you don't hear from him within a couple of days, let us know," Jim Alexander had said on parting. "We'll issue a lookout for him."

Rather than wait and worry for word of his whereabouts, she decided to take a short morning stroll around the block in the hope some fresh morning air would take the edge off her concern. Alas, it didn't work. She arrived back at the office in the same stressed state she left it. So absorbed was she in thought she paid scant attention to the building maintenance man she had called in to take a look at the busted door. "I'm not sure who pays for this...us or the FBI," she said, as she slipped past him.

She walked to her desk, her attention instantly drawn to the flashing red light on her phone messaging system. She sat down, took a deep breath, and pressed the button. The machine's voice informed her that the message had been received ten minutes prior.

"Hello, Tamra. It's Adam. In case you haven't been able to get hold of me, I wanted to let you know we're still on the road in search of Mr. Coulter. Right now, we're in a little town called Saint-Raphael. We've made some progress and hope to wrap this thing up in the next day or so. Hope things are going fine on your end. Tell my daughter not to worry. I'll be home for her big night coming up. Bye for now."

She paused a few moments to collect her thoughts, then shouted in delight. "Yes!" causing the maintenance man to stick his head inside the opened doorway. "Did you just win the lottery?" he asked.

"Yes...yes I did," she said. "I just won the lottery."

———

But did she? As was often her custom when seeking a little downtime in the middle of the day, she decided to spend her lunch break relaxing to the sights and sounds of Tampa's downtown waterfront district. Following a short trek along the river, she settled into a favorite bench of hers in one of the quieter sections of the area where passersby were few and far between, even on a day as refreshing as the one she was experiencing. It was not so much the azure blue skies, puffy white clouds, and rustling of palm trees that engaged her as it was the balm of the fragrant scent wafting in on a steady tropical breeze. Not far from where she parked herself sat a nursery. When the wind was right, the unmistakable perfume of frangipani permeated the air, a surefire elixir to calm her anxieties.

Yes, she had anxieties—lingering ones—despite the good news about Adam. In her lap rested an opened book of classic English poetry, a handy prop she would bury her head in to discourage passing strangers from striking up unsolicited conversations. Often, as on this occasion, she would scan the opened page and mindlessly peruse the contents. Presently, a last line from one of the entries caught her attention. "They also serve who only stand and wait," it read. She recalled from her school days how its meaning perplexed the class. "John Milton was a minister," the instructor explained. "Religious matters were a central theme of his works. At the time, he was going blind and thus the title of the poem, *On His Blindness*. He believed his worsening condition foreshadowed an end to his writing and consequently his ability to serve his God. Yet, within the divine world he operated, he realized it was not an end, thus his conclusion, 'They also serve who only stand and wait.'"

It may have been the author's religious inclination that gave birth to the line, but Tamra could not help but draw a secular parallel to her current situation. Unlike Milton she had no physical disability, but could it be a blindness of another kind that led her to her present state? "It's not what you think," he had said of his trip to Colorado. Well, what was it she was supposed to think? He freely admitted from the beginning he was also seeing another woman. It was not like he was making a big secret out of it. Nonetheless, was it not a clear sign of whose interest was uppermost in his mind? Where did that leave her? Adam was a good boss, a good man, a good father, and no doubt a good catch, most women would say. From the outset she recognized his hesitancy to cross the professional divide and take up a personal relationship with a subordinate. She, nonetheless, welcomed it. Could he now be having second thoughts regarding the propriety of the relationship? She had much to be thankful for at this stage of her life, yet the promise of a family life, the one missing ingredient to a fulfilling one for her, appeared to be drifting out of her reach. One thing was certain. She would never view this as a competition. Being herself was all anyone could ask of her. If that wasn't enough, then on to the next stage for all involved.

"Goliath...settle down!" an elderly lady shouted to her feisty bulldog, as she walked him along the path aside the river. "He's always like this around here...must be something in the water," the lady remarked to the young woman on the bench with the book in hand, drawing a nod and a smile from her.

Tamra closed the book of poetry and returned to work, prepared to stand and wait for whatever future awaited her.

CHAPTER THIRTEEN

THE CHURCH GARDEN SURVIVED THE STORM AS WELL AS COULD BE expected, the gardener concluded, looking out over the rows of crops. Other than a scattering of wind-blown limbs, leaves, and produce, the damage was limited, a result he credited to the line of cedar trees he had planted a few years back along the perimeter of the grounds that served as a windbreak. The taller plants he had wrapped in sheets of burlap for additional protection. As for water damage, it also was limited. Again his loss prevention measures proved to be effective. He had both raised the beds of the plants and added more layers of mulch to protect the more vulnerable crops. In addition, he had dug out trenches to drain the storm water runoff.

He stepped back for another view of the field. Yes, his garden for the most part was intact and ripe for further growth. It already covered nearly a half-acre of ground and there was room for more, since the church grounds spread over two acres of land. The pastor advised him some time back he could extend the garden—not only advised him but encouraged him. The pastor's vision for it turned out to be as grand as his. It was intended to become a compact fruit and vegetable farm whose produce would provide the community a steady source of foods.

"We will christen it the David Coulter Community Garden," the pastor one day said in a playful tone.

From its inception members of the church community had been actively involved in the project, volunteering their time and effort to grow the garden. The original idea for it was planted in his head by Father Jude on the first day he walked into the pastor's tiny office unannounced and asked if there was anything in the way of chores he could help him with. The timing could not have been better. The pastor presented to him his long-held dream of building a garden on the church grounds in the tradition of the historical plantation gardens. The pastor went on to explain that long before the country was liberated from the French, plantation owners granted their slaves plots of land on which to plant their gardens. Eventually, they became more than just simple garden projects.

Utilizing a combination of native and African farming practices they had brought with them from their ancestral land, slaves were able to grow enormous amounts of produce efficiently and, most importantly, effectively in that they were able to sustain the production. In addition to staples like rice and corn that later formed the basis of the Haitian diet, they added a variety of vegetables such as tomatoes and cabbage, as well as a variety of tropical fruits. Melons, peanuts, and other West African crops were also popular. Altogether, the mix established a continuity of indigenous farming practices among the peasants. Plantation owners looked favorably on this development, Father Jude explained, not out of some great magnanimity on their part, but because it allowed them to pass on the responsibility for food production to the slaves, who exercised total control over their small plots of land. In addition, if the garden turned out to be productive, the slaves could sell whatever remainder there was at the local markets and apply the profits to buying their freedom.

Water for the garden project was an issue from the beginning, especially during persistent dry periods. To meet the need, he drew on two sources. One was a working well dug for the community by an international aid organization that was able to overcome logistical hurdles to get trucks to the area to carry out the task. A second was a nearby river. During the dry spells, women of the parish volunteered to lug large jugs of the precious resource on top of their heads from the small stream to the garden, a distance of half a mile. Seeing the long processions, one right after the other, was a wonder to behold, not to mention a lifesaver to the plants.

Yes, the garden project initially gave him a new purpose in life, something fundamentally good to which he could devote the remainder of his life. He would be growing life, and in so doing, perhaps be offering a small measure of compensation for the life he took. It sounded reasonable at the time, but little by little the heaviness of his guilt would always creep back, borne on a memory he knew would never fade, much less die.

He once again surveyed the scene. The garden had weathered the storm, alright, an outcome he was not entirely confident of the moment the first gusts of wind and rain came howling down the mountains. Pleased with its resiliency, he commenced with the cleanup effort, removing the burlap from around the taller plants. He next began the process of removing all of the debris strewn about the field. Normally, he would have volunteers coming to his assistance, but the locals were busy cleaning debris from around their own homes.

"This is…what is the phrase in English…a metaphor for life?" the pastor called out from across the way, as he cleared debris from the perimeter of the church itself. "Much like a garden, man needs constant care and attention, if he is to survive the storms of life."

No offense to the pastor, but his observation reminded Coulter of those who found a metaphor of life in nearly every activity under the sun. How often had he heard during the course of his football career that the game was a metaphor for life; how the rules of the contest are clearly defined in contrast to a society where rules often disappear in a legal fog; how the success of a team depends on each member fulfilling their individual responsibilities, and how there's always the chance of turning a sure loss into a win with that last desperate Hail Mary? Nonetheless, it's a game we're talking about, he reaffirmed to himself.

Just as the monastic life is a retreat from the world, games are a retreat from life. In sport there is always that next game or next season to mitigate the loss you suffered. Not so in life where the stakes are much higher, where there are no mitigating circumstances for the loss of a daughter due directly to your gross negligence.

Nonetheless, by his own account, he had survived the stages of grief his therapist advised would confront him for who knows how long, starting with the mind-numbing shock of the event itself, followed in turn by the denial it even occurred, by the impulse to replay the scenario over and over to determine what he might have done differently, by an intense yearning to have had a few more minutes of life to tell her how much he loved her, by the weight of the guilt, by the anger over how others could go on with their lives as if nothing had happened when he knew damn well their emotions were simmering beneath the surface, and finally by the fading hope that everything could be fixed with a little understanding on his part.

At last, drained of all hope, he decided his only recourse was to seek redemption, something he planned on doing by growing the parish garden. Not long after settling into the married life, prior to his becoming a father, he took gardening up as a hobby, enrolling in and completing a Master Gardener program sponsored by the local county extension service. Little did he realize at the time how important a role it would play in his later life. The church garden would become his personal Eden where the material world met the spiritual and whose bounty he would share with the community. He was convinced of his ability to turn it into the small farm he and the pastor envisioned, one capable of supplying the local populace a reliable source of food. He would make it an example for all of the parishes of the country. Perhaps it would bring a little order, not only to the chaos in his life but to that of others as well.

He paused in his cleanup to peruse a final time the sun-drenched landscape. It was not like he had made no effort toward redemption before. It was just that every time he felt like he was taking a step toward feeling whole again, the entire process would collapse under the weight of the horrible reality that was his, much like a struggling seedling having the life snuffed out of it by the weight of a mammoth mudslide. Nor was his garden sanctuary immune to outside forces. Sooner or later, an intruder was bound to arrive and threaten to burst his cocoon, of that he was certain, just as he was certain it wouldn't be a force of nature doing the intruding.

CHAPTER FOURTEEN

Of all the potential problems Adam and Pierre faced on the road, this one they should have expected. The town of Saint-Raphael had no gas stations. The oversight sent them scurrying for advice from the locals on how to deal with the predicament. "Oh, it happens quite often," one resident informed Pierre. "The man you need to see is Jonas Ador. He has a garage a quarter mile down the road from here. Look for the blue and white building."

It came to pass Jonas was an enterprising fellow. Every month he would drive to Milot and load up on gasoline—large canisters of it—to bring back to his garage where he would wait on ill-prepared travelers to come calling. Needless to say, the mark-up price was exorbitant. "Hey, who can blame him?" Pierre asked, following their fill-up. "He's only following the basic law of supply and demand."

They checked Dr. Damaur's map and headed off to continue their search. Saint-Raphael sat in a valley, bordered by high mountains, at least high by Haitian standards. The city itself was mainly comprised of single-level houses constructed of concrete blocks covered with stucco. The most distinguishing feature of the homes was how closely together they were clustered. There was scant room between them.

"There are no building codes here, apparently," Adam noted.

"But they do have electricity," Pierre said in response. "How many Third-World nations don't?"

They had the secondary road they were on nearly to themselves. Cars were few and far between. Aside from the motor bikes, foot traffic, and the occasional donkey rider, they were the show.

"This section of town couldn't be more barren," Adam noted, as they approached the northern edge of the city.

"Reminds me of those small towns along the gulf coast of Mexico my wife and I would visit…dirt streets, draining heat, drab buildings, a few chickens and dogs running around loose, and a donkey or two. Add a few hitching posts, several mangy horses, a cantina, and you have the setting of a south-of-the-border shoot-'em-up."

"What were you and your wife doing traveling the Mexican gulf coast?"

"She had a lot of Spanish blood in her, spoke the language, and like me, enjoyed traveling off the beaten path. She claimed that to better understand the culture, you had to mingle with the locals."

"What did you learn from the mingling?"

"I learned small towns worldwide have much in common. Like here in Haiti, there is little or no government presence in the rural areas, so families tend to themselves and rely on their neighbors for help when needed. How about you, Adam…you originally a small town guy?"

"Yes, I grew up in a tiny one called Strawberry Hills in the north central part of Florida."

"You have family there?"

"Yes, my parents still reside there. They are getting up in age and keeping up the house is becoming a burden for them. They talk of downsizing and getting a condo but are reluctant to give up the home they've lived in for their entire married life. My efforts to talk them into moving to Tampa have met with no success thus far."

"What did they make of you becoming a single father?"

"They were very supportive. For selfish reasons, they confessed. They wanted a grandchild in the worst way. The fact it was by way of adoption came as a surprise to them, though in the end no less rewarding. Noelle turned out to be as great an addition to their lives as she was to mine. She is the lure I use in trying to talk them into making the move to the city."

"What brought you to the big city?"

"The same thing that brought the masses to them...jobs. I went to work for a private investigator in Tampa and when he retired, I took over the operation at his urging."

"That was your childhood dream...to become a private eye?"

"No, not at all. I stumbled into it. One day I saw a help wanted notice in the paper and thought 'Hey, that might be interesting.' So, off to the city I went."

"The ad was in the Strawberry Hills paper?"

"No, I happened to be on a weekend trip to Tampa to visit a friend and while there picked up a paper to check the ads."

"My grandfather back in Louisiana would always say the great American migration was not the movement westward, nor the flight from the farm to the city, but the movement from the front porch to the living room, brought about by the boob tube."

"He swore off TV?"

"No, his family was the first one on the block to get one. Their house soon became the hub of the neighborhood. Every night they would have several neighbors stop by to sit in the living room and marvel at the contraption."

"Tell me, Pierre, when you were traveling those remote towns in Mexico, did you ever spot any late model blue Chevy cars on the streets?"

Adam's reference drew a puzzled look from his companion. "You mean like the one your friend Colby Flint drives?"

"Yeah, like the one up ahead of us parked alongside the street."

Pierre trained his eyes on the spot. "Well, I'll be damned. Do you suppose he's in it...couldn't belong to anyone else," he said, slowing the Land Rover.

At that moment, the driver's side window of the Chevy was lowered and out flew a cigarette butt to join the pile of other discards on the ground.

"Pull up behind him," Adam instructed.

Pierre eased the Land Rover to a stop, whereupon Adam hopped from the car, stepped to the side of the Chevy, opened the front door, and slid into the passenger seat.

"Mr. Fraley, welcome aboard," Flint said, firing up another nicotine stick.

"What are you doing here?" Adam asked directly.

"Waiting for you."

"How did you know I was here?"

"A nice lady doctor at the hospital told me late yesterday you were headed this way. I'll have you know I spent the entire night slogging my way down here. I've never had so much fun on the open road."

"So, she divulged private medical information?"

"What medical information? I simply asked her if she knew where I could find a dear old friend and compatriot of mine, Adam Fraley, and she kindly told me."

"How long have you been waiting?"

"An hour or so. I first had to take care of an unexpected delay in the hospital parking lot, followed by a visit to the local police station, thanks to you. And to think I was minding my own business before all hell broke loose."

"You were minding your own business? You sure it wasn't a case of you minding other people's business?"

"Listen, I was waiting for an old acquaintance of mine to finish his hospital stay when this blue-clad storm trooper came charging out to accuse me of assaulting an American tourist. I can't imagine who planted that idea in his head...can you?" he asked, turning to face his front seat visitor for the first time.

"The fact is you survived the episode and are now here," Adam stated. "The question is...for what?"

"To make a deal."

"What kind of a deal?"

"My silence for your silence," Flint said, exhaling a drag, "a straight up tit for tat deal."

"Do you mind if I crack this window? The air is getting a little thick in here."

"Help yourself, though I do have the air on in case you didn't notice. This Haitian sun is much like Florida's when it comes to dispensing the heat."

Adam lowered the window. "Okay, silence for silence…explain."

"You're on your way to see Mr. Coulter. For your information, I've already seen him. And by the way, he's just a half mile further on up this road."

"Did you talk to him?" Adam anxiously asked.

"Don't worry yourself. I said I saw him. I didn't talk to him."

"Did he see you?"

"Nope, and here's where the deal comes in. On the one hand, I could make a return trip to the church, warn Coulter he is about to be outed by a private detective working out of Tampa and that it's all a scam to upend his present life."

"You think he's going to buy into that, not even knowing who you are and what the hell you're talking about?"

"Chances are he won't, but it will instill enough caution in him to outright disregard anything you might have to say to him. Right?"

"I wouldn't be so sure about that."

"I am sure, Fraley. It's plain he's a guy who doesn't want to be found or else why would everyone be hiring private eyes to track him down? Hell, I don't even know what everyone is after him for, nor do I care at this point. It's likely he's not in the mood to cooperate with you in the first place. A visit from me would only guarantee it."

"Suppose I put a stop to your trip."

"Physically? Come on, Fraley. We're both soft boiled, not hard boiled. The physical confrontation option is not in our genes."

"Two more minutes of this conversation and one of us is likely to become hard boiled."

"I repeat, it's not in your genes."

"Then why do I have twenty-five stitches sewn across my chest?"

"Oh, so that was the reason for your stay in the hospital. Well, I'm sure it wasn't you who initiated the confrontation. I still hold to my point."

"Okay, what's the other end of the deal?" Adam asked, reluctantly conceding the point about his ability to throw a monkey wrench into the search.

The attention of both suddenly was drawn to an elderly man who had stepped out from the shadow of a scarred cinder block building and was ambling toward the Chevy. Flint immediately snatched his package of cigarettes from atop the dashboard, jacked one up, and reached out the window and offered it to the guy. The old man took it and without a word returned from whence he came. "He's the third guy this morning who's stopped by for one," Flint said.

"Good to see you dispensing aid to the impoverished," Adam gibed.

"Hey, anything to help them get through the day," Flint responded.

"Back to the deal," Adam directed.

"Okay, I admit I took this job not knowing who I was dealing with," Flint continued. "Not a wise thing to do, but I needed the work and screening applicants is a luxury I don't have the time and resources to do. I was simply hired for the purpose of locating this guy Coulter here in Haiti. The higher ups somehow got wind you were also tracking him. Tailing you in the hope of locating him was a midstream tactic."

"Who sent the goon after me?"

"I didn't know there was a goon."

"How do you think I ended up in that medical facility—or the hospital as you call it?"

"I wasn't sure why," Flint said with a shrug of the shoulders. "I received word from a higher up you were in there recuperating from an accident and was given instructions to tail you when you were released. Come to think of it, sending a goon after you didn't make much sense if it was you who was going to lead me to Coulter. No wonder the guy who gave me the instructions sounded pissed. The goon must have gotten his instructions mixed up, or maybe since he failed at the job, tailing you was the next best thing."

"Who was the higher up who gave you the instructions to tail me?"

"I have no idea. He simply identified himself as the field coordinator for the operation. Nasty fellow, though. He ended the last call by telling me he would personally slice my tongue out if for any reason I talked to the authorities about all this."

"Who was the man who hired you?"

"A guy named Warnick."

"So, let's hear the rest of your proposed deal. You won't interfere with my meeting with Coulter if I do what?"

"Like I said, I considered this a simple tracking job. As things progressed, I learned my client might be involved in a big-time overseas insurance scam and the whole thing was about to be blown up by the FBI."

"Who told you this?"

"I do have some sources, Fraley, one of them in the FBI. I don't know what the fallout will be, but if the FBI does come calling on you, it would serve me well if you told them as far as you know, I did nothing illegal, that I was hired by this phantom outfit to do some simple surveillance on you and had no idea it had anything to do with criminal fraud."

"Why don't you ask your source in the department to relay that?"

"I don't want him exposed."

Flint reached into his back pocket and pulled out a billfold. From it he plucked a photo and flashed it to Adam. "My wife and two kids," he said. "I thought you'd like to see a picture of them."

"Okay, I'll ask you directly, Flint. Did you have any idea criminal activity was involved in this case?"

"I do now, but not then."

Adam knew how it was for a cash-strapped, one-person operation. Not to excuse them, but often they would take on a case unaware of how far the tentacles of it reached. It was easy for them to get in over their head. He believed this to be the case with Flint.

"You got a deal, Flint. Consider your Haitian vacation ended."

"You call this a vacation...stuck in the middle of nowhere with my travel expenses now all on me? Some vacation—more like a penance."

Flint's analogy drew a smile from Adam. "Look at it this way... you're contributing to the economy of an impoverished nation."

"By handing out smokes to the locals?"

"Consider yourself a missionary to the poor."

"I'm a missionary who's got twenty-four hours to get the hell out of the country, courtesy of you."

"They're kicking you out?"

"You better believe it," he declared. "Time for me to get out of this business anyway, Fraley. It's not a good fit for me."

"Have you got a better one in mind?"

"You're damn right I do…the cadaver transportation business."

"The what?"

"The cadaver transportation business," he repeated with verve. "Here's how it works…"

"I really don't have time to listen, Flint. We've got our own business to tend to at the moment."

"You mean Coulter? Hell, he ain't going anywhere. Why don't I just give you the basics and then you can be on your way. I'm telling you this business is going to take off. It might be something you will want to look into, unless you'd rather traipse around these Third World countries and end up spending time in jails or hospitals."

"What makes you think it's going to take off?"

"Because the demand is going to skyrocket, Fraley. It won't be long before all these baby boomers start dying off in big numbers. In fact, it's already begun. There are going to be more corpses riding around in cars than live bodies. The streets are going to be the scene of one big funeral procession after another."

"Isn't that the business of funeral homes?" Adam asked, glancing at the rearview mirror to look for signs of Pierre getting restless.

"They only control a portion of the market. For example, they don't transport corpses to organ donation centers or to morgues for autopsies. And what about all those who have no relatives or anyone else willing to make funeral arrangements for them? The hospitals want to move the dead out ASAP. The bottom line is a lot of the transporting of the dead from one point to the other doesn't involve hospitals or funeral homes."

"I thought cremation was the wave of the future."

Flint hesitated, as though he hadn't considered it. "Well…maybe, but in the meantime…"

"In the meantime, why don't you simply get a job driving a hearse?" Adam asked, cutting him short.

"And be a low wage-earner having to listen to some stupid boss, or worse yet, a phantom boss like I am now? No thanks."

"You're going to do your own driving?"

"Sure…why not? All you need is a simple license to do business, a driver's license, a reliable van—though some prefer a refrigerated box truck—a gurney, a few spare body bags in case one is needed, and a comfortable attitude working with corpses."

"It's not like they're going to complain…is it?"

"Right…nice and quiet atmosphere with no back talk, though one guy in the business told me he once heard a low guttural moan coming from one corpse he was transporting that nearly sent him through the roof."

"He had a live one?"

"Nah, it was due to a carbon dioxide buildup in the lungs, he was later told."

"I think I'll stick with my present job, Flint, but best of luck to you. Now, if you don't mind, I'll be on my way."

Adam reached for the door handle when Flint stopped him. "Say, Fraley, just what is the story with this guy Coulter?"

"Unless you want to risk violating your twenty-four-hour deadline, I would postpone hearing it, Colby. It's a long story."

"Well then, you're right. Maybe we can cover it over a beer once we're both back in Florida."

"What's he up to?" Pierre asked upon his cohort's return.

"He's been kicked out of the country and is on his way home."

"Kicked out for what?"

"For assaulting me, a respectable tourist. I identified him as my attacker back at the hospital."

"Aha! So that was the story behind his sudden disappearance you were going to tell me about but never did. Is he over it?"

"He's getting there."

They watched Flint pull the Chevy onto the road, heading it in the direction of the church.

"You sure he's headed out of the country?" Pierre anxiously asked.

"Surely, he's not going back on his word," Adam whispered to himself. He was about to direct Pierre to get after him, when the Chevy slowed and began a U-turn. As Flint passed the Land Rover, the two could not help but notice the Cheshire cat smile attached to his face.

"He seems to be having fun," Pierre said.

"No, he's a tormented soul," Adam sarcastically replied, before turning his attention to the road ahead. "Let's go. Time to engage David Coulter."

———

Much in the manner of other houses of worship in Haiti, St. Joseph's stood as the centerpiece of the local community. "Most buildings in the country, especially the residences, are constructed without the benefit of engineers or architects," Pierre noted on their approach to the parish. "Not so the churches, they're given a prominent place in most communities. It goes to show how deep the religious feelings are among the people."

St. Joseph's was built atop a fairly steep rise. It was a simple, all-white structure of modest size and design, topped by a soaring steeple. If engineers and architects were involved in its building, they were displaying great restraint. What stood out the most to Adam and Pierre aside from the steeple was not so much the architecture of the church, but a terraced garden that covered nearly half the slope leading up to the structure. "That thing's the size of half a football field," Adam observed as they pulled to a stop at the base of the hill. "It could feed the entire parish."

"It wouldn't surprise me if it did," Pierre said, shutting down the engine. "Church gardens here are considered community gardens. It's a way for the churches to connect with the parishioners on a serviceable level."

At the moment, there were two men working the grounds. One looked to be a Haitian priest from the garb he wore…cream-colored short-sleeve shirt, tab collar, and maroon slacks. They presumed him to be Dr. Damaur's brother, Father Jude, who was busy picking up storm-tossed debris from the periphery of the church. The other worker was a white, middle-aged guy dressed in powder blue clothing that could easily pass for hospital scrubs. A straw hat protected him from the blinding sunshine bearing down on the section of garden he was clearing of limbs and twigs.

"There's your David Coulter…risen from the dead," Pierre said. "Do you suppose he's the sole architect and keeper of this garden? If he is, he must have spent his entire self-imposed exile working on it."

Before exiting the car, a last-minute option popped into Adam's mind. They had found Coulter. That was the task he had taken on. Would it not be better to let Carolina take it from here? He could return to Tampa, advise her of their discovery and return with her in tow to this very spot. How better an emissary for the family would she be than he? But then he recalled her specific request to "put my family back together again." It was crunch time and he was obligated to fulfill his end of the bargain…was he not? Why place the burden back on her? Annoyed by his moment of indecision, he shoved open the car door.

"Let's do it," he said. "Why don't you go entertain the priest while I have a chat with Mr. Coulter," Adam suggested on the trek up.

"You mean get out my deck of cards and show him some tricks?"

"Maybe something more engaging to him, like hearing about your obsession with his sister."

"I believe you have the object of my affections confused, my friend, or are you suffering from a short-memory loss?"

"My memory is intact," Adam reassured him.

They took a wooden stairway leading up the slope. Halfway up, Adam stepped off onto the row of terrace Coulter was working. Pierre continued on up toward the church to engage the priest.

Coulter no doubt had seen their arrival. Two Caucasian guys who were not here to pick up some cucumbers, he probably thought at first sight.

The transition from the indoor world of high finance to the outdoor one of gardening had had a noticeable effect on Coulter's physical appearance, Adam noted on his approach. Granted, he only had a photo to judge by, but it was enough to gauge the change in the man's upper body condition. The head, shoulders, and arms all appeared sturdier and the face more weathered. The forearms, in particular, had a jackhammer tone to them, presumably developed over recent years by his wielding of the tools of his new trade. Despite his advancing age, it looked as though the former tight end could once again take on NFL defenders.

"Mr. Coulter," Adam called out, momentarily drawing the man's attention away from the debris he was clearing from the plant beds. "My name is Adam Fraley. I'm a private investigator your daughter hired to locate you," he said, foregoing any preliminary small talk.

Coulter returned his attention to the soil and the limbs and twigs he was gathering along a row of cabbage plants. "So, you found me," he said in a matter-of-fact manner, as though that indeed was the easy part.

"She would like for you to return home."

"This is my home."

"Your home or your place of penance?"

A look of annoyance immediately formed on his ruddy face. "Look, Mr. Fraley, don't take this personally, but my life is none of your business."

"Your daughter made it my business."

"To find me...so, you did. Congratulations, now you can return home."

"Long way to come to go home empty-handed," Adam said, folding his arms as he casually observed Coulter at work. "You tell me...how should I pass the word on to her that you have no interest in returning?"

Coulter took a handful of twigs and stuffed them in a trash bag he was trailing behind him. "I'm not going to address that question with someone who has no idea of the circumstances surrounding my coming here."

"Oh yeah? Does the priest up there talking to my friend have any idea of the circumstances that brought you here? I'm thinking there's a good chance I know more about those circumstances than he does. Maybe it would be best for everyone if he's made aware of them. You know...get all the facts out on the table before a decision is made."

Coulter cast a quick glance at the two who appeared actively engaged in happy talk, before ignoring the question.

"Didn't think so," Adam said. "Before you worry about the next life, maybe you should start worrying about this one."

It may have been a harsh opening salvo he had directed at Coulter, but Adam had made up his mind long beforehand he wasn't going to humor the man. He figured the guy already had had plenty of compassionate verbiage thrown at him during all of his therapy sessions and look where it had gotten him.

"I'm in no way, shape, or form trying to become a saint, if that's what you're getting at," Coulter declared, taking off his hat and wiping his brow with the back of his hand. "I've found my calling and it's not what you think."

"Good to hear. I don't know of any saint who inflicted on their family the kind of pain you have…and the worse kind…the mental pain. As for your calling, it's plain to see. You are more interested in cultivating your garden than your family."

"Mr. Fraley, until you experience anything close to what I experienced with my baby daughter, I suggest you hold your opinions to yourself."

"Mr. Coulter, I also have a young daughter, and if I did experience anything with her that was close to what you experienced, I would own it. I certainly wouldn't run from it. And do I need to remind you there's another daughter in your life as well as a wife you are running from?"

"I'm not running from anything or anybody."

"Oh, I forgot. You're doing your penance. Well, here's Father Fraley's suggestion for a better penance…be a father to your family and quit hiding from your guilt. The truth is you'll have to forgive yourself before anyone else will."

"Forgive myself? Look, detective, you don't need to play the role of Good Samaritan with me. I'll take care of my own problems."

"There have been many others who've experienced and overcome unimaginable personal tragedies, Mr. Coulter. It's not like you're a trailblazer in this regard. I would think you'd take a measure of comfort from their struggles. As impossible as it seemed for them, somehow their path in life took a positive turn despite the obstacles."

Coulter set aside his work to face his inquisitor. "The only positive aspect to my life at the moment, Mr. Fraley, is that the remaining months of it are spinning down the drain like the last remnants of a tub full of dirty water."

"Then what good is the penance if you are looking forward to its end? Seems to me you would want to extend it...make sure you have enough on the record to compensate for your transgression. Everything has an end to it, Mr. Coulter, penance as well as life. Does it matter which end comes first for you—or are they so inseparable in your mind, one can't exist without the other?"

Coulter returned to work, ignoring the question.

Adam thought a moment before continuing. "Once, long ago, I was the beneficiary of a Good Samaritan who helped get me and my mother out of a difficult situation on a remote highway. He declined my mother's monetary offer for his effort, saying there would come a time when we could return the favor. Little did I know when the time came it would be to the same Samaritan."

Coulter lifted his eyes from his debris-gathering to cast a lingering look at Adam and then at the sky. His mind was in rewind but apparently it didn't score a hit. If it did, he was not letting on to it. Instead, he returned his attention to his chores.

"Okay...have it your way. You can stay here and sulk your life away. I, on the other hand, am headed home. As you pointed out, my part is done with," Adam said in a measured tone. "As a last resort, I thought we just might force you to go...maybe club you over the head, throw you into the car, and lug you back with us. Now I realize that knocking you over the head is likely to be no more effective than trying to knock sense into it." Adam unfolded his arms, ceding his relaxed manner. "There is, however, one last matter to take care of now that you've decided to stay." He reached into his back pocket and pulled out the picture of Carolina he carried with him, handing it to her father. "She wrote you a message on the back of it."

Coulter took the photo and contemplated it for a moment, before flipping it over to read the message on the backside.

Dad, so proud to have been your daughter.
   Love, Carolina

Adam stepped past Coulter and walked briskly toward the stairway. "Hey, Pierre!" he called out. "Saddle up, we're going home!"

"If the boss man says it's time to go...it's time to go," he called back, excusing himself from the company of Father Jude.

CHAPTER FIFTEEN

Morning broke bright over Tampa, an overnight cool front having muscled away a lingering overcast. He was once again back in his pickup, traveling paved roads and knowing where he was going, except at the moment he didn't. Tamra had given him Carolina Coulter's address, but he was having difficulty locating it until a helpful gas station attendant pointed him in the right direction. Minutes later he was knocking on the door of a late-model, second-floor condo on the south side of town.

"Adam," she said, upon opening the door. "What a surprise. What brings you here?"

"Grab your purse. We're going for a ride."

"To where?"

"You'll see."

She took a moment to retrieve her purse and keys, locking the unit's door behind her, before bounding down the steps with him to his truck.

"When did you get back?" she asked, as he maneuvered through traffic.

"Early this morning."

"Can't wait to hear your report."

"I'm saving it for later. How's the public relations job going?"

"Fine," she said, accepting his switch to small talk. "It's all about building up credibility for the firm. They seem to think I'm doing a competent job."

"What kind of firm?"

"Finance. It's a good thing I minored in the subject in college."

In time, Adam's destination became apparent to his passenger. "Are we going to Queen of Peace?" she asked, seeing the familiar outline of the church come into view.

"Yes," Adam said, turning his truck into the empty parking lot and pulling it to a stop in front of the entrance.

"All the services are over for the day, Adam," she said, puzzled by the move. "The church is empty."

He shut off the engine and paused a moment, before turning to her. "Not entirely, there's someone waiting for you in there."

"Oh my God," she exclaimed breathlessly, realizing the meaning of his message. "I had faith you would find him but to talk him into returning...I had my doubts. What did you say to convince him?"

"It had nothing to do with what I said to him, Carolina. My words had about as much impact as your average politician's stump speech. It's what you said with the message you left on the back of your photo."

Adam recalled the moment when he and Pierre were bounding down the steps from St. Joseph to leave when they heard Coulter shout out to them. "Wait!"

"Perhaps it was not so much what you said but the way you said it," Adam added. "It could have had something to do with tense."

"Tense?"

"Yes...you know...present perfect...future perfect...past perfect... or is it pluperfect? Whatever, my high school English teacher was always drilling into us the importance of tense...how it could impact the meaning of a sentence."

"I don't understand."

"Neither do I," he confessed. "Grammar was a real struggle for me."

She slowly shook her head in disbelief. "Are you coming in with me?" she asked.

"No, my job is over with. It's now up to you and your mother—and your father—to take it from here. There will be a cab coming in about a half hour to take you and your father to your mother's home. I should tell you that John Warnick, the man your mother planned to marry, was at the center of an international insurance scam that was just busted by the FBI. She may not be hearing from him for a while, if ever. According to an FBI official, she likely had no knowledge of it. It was solely a way for Warnick to put forth a normal face while dipping into your mother's financial nest egg."

Carolina reached across the front seat and gave him a hug. "Thank you…thank you so much," she said, prior to hopping from the truck to head for her reunion.

Coulter's decision was not as simple as Adam made it out to be. There were issues to be resolved. Foremost among them was her father's understandable reluctance to walk away from a project to which he was fully committed. The solution took place in the tiny church rectory following Coulter's call to Adam and Pierre to "wait" as they were leaving. The subsequent meeting came at the invitation of Father Jude.

"I cannot simply walk away from this project," Coulter said upfront, throwing on the table for discussion the major obstacle to his leaving.

Father Jude, who had been briefed prior to the sit-down on the issue at hand, early on indicated on which side of the argument he stood. "I know you have a lot invested in this, David, and it will be difficult to replace you, but we will find someone. Family comes first."

The affable pastor had a lilt to his voice that served his mediator role well, Adam observed. Harshness in this instance was an element they could do without.

"Who could that possibly be, Father?" Coulter asked in response to the pastor's reference to a replacement. "There is no one who has the time to carry the project forward. Certainly, you don't."

"Perhaps one of the members of our parish will step forward," the pastor suggested, a note of uncertainty in his voice.

"Father Jude, the parish volunteers already devote as much time as they are able to the project. Any additional volunteering on their part would take away time they should be spending with their own families," Coulter countered.

There it was…the issue threatening to derail Coulter's decision to return home. "Yes…you're right…family first," Adam wanted to say, pointing out the irony in his argument, but didn't. The look in Coulter's eyes already indicated his realization of what he just said. Still, it was evident the man was wavering. He's about to revert to his penitent mode, Adam reckoned at the time, when a white knight in the person of Pierre came forward. "I'll take the project over," he said firmly, surprising all, including Adam.

"You don't even live here," Coulter said, pointing out the obvious.

"I will be soon," he replied. "I have a friend living just south of Milot whom I plan to visit on an extended stay. As I'm sure you know, it's a short distance from here, so I can easily make the commute."

"You have a background in horticulture?" Coulter asked.

"As I mentioned to the pastor earlier today, I come from Cajun country in Louisiana where gardening is a family tradition. So, yes, I do have experience. Maybe not as much as you, but enough to keep your project afloat until a more permanent solution can be found."

"Perhaps David would be willing to return occasionally to keep abreast of the project and offer any advice he might be willing to share," the pastor proposed.

In a small sign he was beginning to be won over, Coulter nodded his assent to the idea.

"Where would you stay?" Adam asked of Pierre with a wry smile.

"He could stay in the caretaker's cottage where David is currently housed," the pastor said, coming to Pierre's aid.

The "cottage" appeared to be more akin to a shed, Adam mused, recalling the small structure with the weathered boards planted adjacent to the church. He pictured the furnishings as a single cot surrounded by shelves stocked with preserves.

A crow squawked its presence, bringing Adam's attention back to the present. He had hung around for a few minutes in the parking lot to bask in the aftermath of the return. By and by, he saw a priest exit the Queen of Peace church from a side door and stroll his way. He rolled down his window. "Father Frank," he said in greeting.

"Hello Adam," the priest said. "You've become a stranger around here. Thankfully, Noelle and her lady friend keep the candle burning."

"How are things going in there?" Adam asked.

"They appear to be going very well."

"I appreciate your keeping the church open a little longer."

"You know, there was a time when the churches were open all day, but that's long past."

"The cab should be arriving shortly. Can you make sure they make it off okay?"

"Sure, and say hello to Noelle for me."

"I'll do that. In fact, I need to take off early from work to help her plan a big event that's coming up this evening."

"A big event...what could that be?"

Adam ignited the engine. "I'm bound to secrecy, Father Frank. Let's just say it may be big enough to bring me back to church one day," he said with a twinkle in his eye.

———

From the church Adam made a beeline to his office. Other than a quick briefing over an airport phone, he had yet to discuss with Tamra the full details of the Coulter case and its aftermath, both on the foreign front as well as the home front.

"Okay, that's one way to implement an open-door policy," he cracked on entering the office, plopping himself down on a chair in front of her desk. "When can we expect it to be replaced?"

"According to the building maintenance guy, in a day or so," she replied, setting aside a stack of unopened mail. "Welcome home. How did it go with Carolina and her father?"

"To be determined. Hopefully, they can work things out."

"What's your sense of it?"

"My sense is they will give it a good shot. As that grand old expression goes...time is a great healer."

"Time is going to be put to the test with this one," she said.

Adam spent the next half hour relating to her the full details of his trip, including his stay in the clinic and the reason for it.

"You say you still have to get your stitches removed?"

"Yes…I'll make an appointment with my doctor before I leave the office today."

He reached out and gently rested his hand on hers. "It's good to be home. I spoke briefly with Jim Alexander and he tells me you were a real trooper."

She shrugged. "You do what you have to do. Where's Pierre?"

"I dropped him off at my place so he could get some rest. I invited him to join us for our little get-together this evening. The guy was a huge help in Haiti."

"How did your trip to Colorado go? she casually asked, as if it were a throwaway question.

"Better than expected, though it seems eons ago," he replied, offering no details.

She probed no further. Her look was one of indifference, the way a person appears when the good and the bad in their life cancel each other out, leaving them back where they were on their long road to fulfillment.

"Anything else?"

"You got a call from Colby Flint. He seemed anxious to talk to you. Is there a problem with him?"

"He thought he might have one with the FBI so he wanted me to put in a good word for him. I did when I spoke with Alexander earlier. Turns out he's got nothing to worry about. I'll give him a call later," he said. "Now, about you and my daughter's ongoing concern. Are you still up for tonight? We could postpone it," he said, hoping to hell she'd stick to her guns.

"And risk the wrath of your daughter?"

"You're right…let's get it over with, so we can move on to something less intense."

"Are you referring to tonight or the Coulter case?"

"Both."

She slipped her hand from beneath his to punch a few computer keys to check what was pending on the schedule. "How about an insurance fraud case?" she asked, scanning the monitor. Adam shook his head no. "A cheating spouse case?" she next asked, drawing a definite no. "Okay, how about an employee background check?"

"Are those all tentative?" he asked.

"At your direction I make everything tentative until it gets your approval," she said.

"Good...then jump the employee background case to the front of the line. We'll deal with the others later." She tapped several more keys.

"Done."

Adam leaned back in his chair. "There...we're back to normal," he said, bringing a grin to her face.

"Adam, when are we ever at normal around here?"

————

Uncle Tony's pizzeria was not simply a brand name to Tamra. Anthony Martini was indeed her uncle, the last living relative of hers. His restaurant was a small, red brick structure located in a middle-class neighborhood of West Tampa, an area populated by a sizable mix of Italian and Cuban families. The furnishings were standard fare...red and white checkerboard tablecloths draped over tables diminutive enough to ensure an intimacy to the dining.

"Maneuvering plates around on a cramped surface lends a family atmosphere to the experience," Tony would always say. For amenities he added a jukebox and pinball machine. For this occasion, he borrowed an extra chair from an adjoining table to accommodate the group of five...Adam, herself, Noelle, Bobby, and Pierre. In the background another Bobby—Bobby Darin—was belting out *Beyond the Sea*, one of her favorites. Family and friends crowded around a table in a relaxing atmosphere, Tamra thought. What could be better? What possibly could go wrong?

"Uncle Tony, why are there no other customers in here?" she called out to him.

"I thought it wise to keep this gathering private," he said, lowering the sound on the jukebox.

She turned to Adam to stir the conversation. "Did you know Bobby was a big Pittsburgh Steelers fan?"

"Oh, is that so?" Adam said, turning his attention to the youngster in question, a fair-haired kid sporting a fresh buzz cut. "Aren't you living down here now?" he asked. "Why are you not a Buccaneers fan?"

Adam felt a sharp kick in the chin from his office manager sitting next to him. "Behave yourself," she whispered in his ear.

"I was just asking," he whispered back.

Tamra was not about to let the conversation take a wrong turn. "Pierre, have you talked to Angeline in Haiti?"

"He's just getting started with the talking," Adam interjected. "He'll have to paint the entire west side of Tampa to pay his next phone bill."

"You may be right," Pierre said, before replying to Tamra, "but to answer your question…yes, I've talked to her."

"I'm so happy for you," she said.

"Say, Tamra, that chair of yours looks sort of wobbly," her uncle called out, as he approached their table. "I think one of the legs is a little shaky. Let me swap it out for another."

"I really haven't noticed a wobble in it," she said, looking down at the legs.

"I want to be sure," he said. "I don't want any insurance claims filed against me."

A soft smile curled her lips. "Uncle Tony, you know I wouldn't do that."

So she stood and let him take the chair. "I'll be back in a moment," he said.

It was an awkward minute for her, standing there waiting for the replacement chair to come. When it didn't, she called out to her uncle. "Uncle Tony?" There was no answer. The growing confusion unsettled her. She so wanted everything to go right this evening. Noelle was counting on her, yet the night was definitely getting off to a stumbling start. She called out to her uncle a second time and again there was no answer. She then turned her attention back to the table. "Something strange is going on…" Abruptly, her hand flew to her mouth on seeing her boss down on one knee in front of her with an open ring box in hand. Her eyes darted around the table…wide smiles all around… knowing smiles for what was about to come.

Adam looked up at her. "And here you thought this evening was going to be all about Noelle and Bobby. No, I hate to disappoint you, Tamra, but this night from the very beginning was intended to be all about you…how special a woman you are…how much my daughter loves you…how much your Uncle Tony loves you…and how Pierre has come to understand the depth of that love. Bobby, I'm not so sure about…he may be wanting to get the hell out of here for all I know," he said, adding a bit of mirth to the occasion before continuing. "I don't mean to diminish all the love the others have for you, but the sum of it could never match my love for you." He took a deep breath. "So, here comes the question…will you marry me?"

Overwhelmed by the suddenness of it, Tamra looked aside for a moment to let her thoughts catch up with her emotions.

"You're not looking for the fire alarm, are you?" he asked.

She turned back to face him. "No, Adam. I'm not looking for the fire alarm and the answer is yes."

Her response set off a celebration at the table. Noelle giddily clapped her hands, while Uncle Tony rushed back with Tamra's chair. He followed with two bottles of champagne, filling everyone's glass, including Noelle's and Bobby's. In minutes, an extra-large pizza was set before them, a Tony Martini special they had no trouble maneuvering around the table.

So, Adam Fraley's Private Investigations was about to become a mom and pop operation. And Bobby? Well, he didn't want to get the hell out of there at all. He was on his third glass of champagne before Uncle Tony decided to cut him off to everyone's relief.

"Well, Pete, any advice going forward?" he asked in a late-night call to the Keys following his engagement party.

"Marriage changes things, Adam. So do engagements."

"I've been told mom and pop operations require a continual back and forth between the personal and the professional, both at home and the office. You have some experience along these lines what with the scrimshaw shop you and Jill have been operating down there. What's your take?"

"You and Tamra already have an on-going personal and professional relationship. Build on the existing one. It appears to be working just fine."

"But you say an engagement can change things. Maybe the old ways no longer apply."

"Okay, if you insist, here are two bits of advice I have for you. First, always put the love you two have for each other above all issues that may arise."

Adam considered the notion. "Not bad, Pete, not bad at all. Maybe your best advice yet. And the second?"

"The second is the precondition for the first. Offer her half ownership in the business."

With the words came the hint of a mischievous smile planted on the face of his mentor.

"So glad I called you."

"Anytime."

POSTSCRIPT

December 15, 1996

Hello Adam,

Greetings from Haiti (and please excuse the handwriting). I have good news to report. Angeline and I are now engaged. My proposal was far less dramatic than yours, my friend. It took place in the church garden, next to the tomato plants. Attach whatever significance you want to the locale, keeping in mind it could as easily have taken place next to the carrots, or cucumbers, or even the turnips. At the moment, I am inside Angeline's store, taking a break from decorating a Christmas tree cut from a nearby hill. Meanwhile, she is outside rotating the tires on her truck. Okay, you can quit your chuckling. I have not given up my manhood. I did change the oil for her the other day.

Mr. Coulter and his wife came for a visit a while back. The atmosphere during it was in stark contrast to when we last met him here. He was pleased with the upkeep of the garden and looked upon it as he would an old friend. He couldn't wait to get his hands dirty, offering to help with the day's tilling. He's not all the way back mentally but he's getting there. He even talked a little football, which to me was a good sign. In the bigger picture, the idea of adding a garden on church property is spreading among the parishes here. Several have begun them with a number of others expressing an interest in doing so. With this in mind, Angeline and I have decided to make our home here for the foreseeable future. Her father passed away two weeks ago, relieving her of the primary responsibility that bound her here. Still, all things considered, we have concluded we could best contribute to the world by applying whatever talents we possess to this little corner of this little nation.

Meanwhile, we have been compiling a wish list. At the top is the desire for you and Tamra to pay us a visit. If not feasible on your end, perhaps we could make it a joint venture, like meeting in Gainesville next year for a Florida Gator Spring football game. What better way to introduce her to American culture? (Okay, enough of male fantasizing.)

One final note: At the suggestion of Angeline and with the permission of the pastor, we held a little christening ceremony during Mr. Coulter's visit. St. Joseph Church's garden is now officially known as the Sadie Coulter Memorial Garden, so stated on the homemade signpost we crafted and planted in the middle of it (photo on the way to you).

Okay, time for me to get back to my decorating.

From Haiti, with warmest regards,
  Pierre and Angeline
  Jwaye Nwel!

THE END

———

Don't miss out on your next favorite book!

Join the Melange Books mailing list at
www.melange-books.com/mail.html

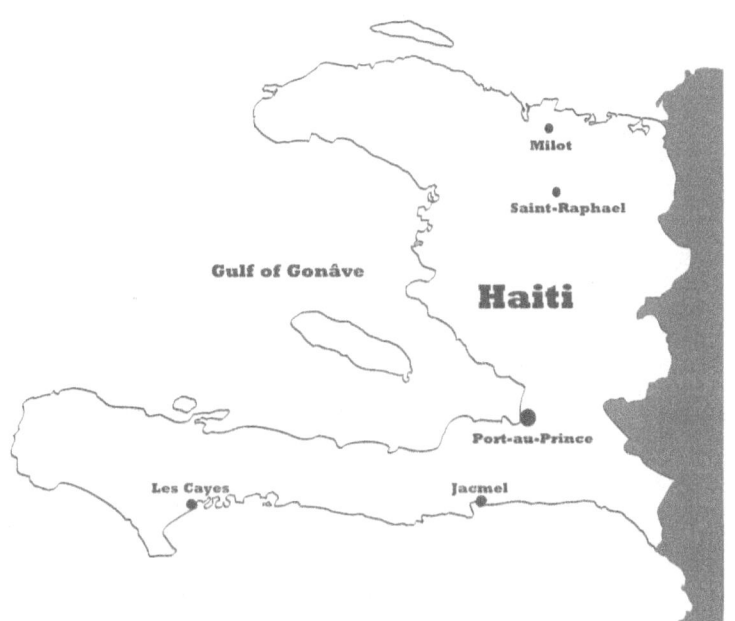

Gulf of Gonâve

Haiti

Milot

Saint-Raphael

Port-au-Prince

Les Cayes

Jacmel

ACKNOWLEDGMENTS

Special thanks to Barbara Whelehan for her assistance in the preparation of the manuscript.

THANK YOU FOR READING

Did you enjoy this book?

We invite you to leave a review at the website of your choice, such as Goodreads, Amazon, Barnes & Noble, etc.

DID YOU KNOW THAT LEAVING A REVIEW...

- Helps other readers find books they may enjoy.
- Gives you a chance to let your voice be heard.
- Gives authors recognition for their hard work.
- Doesn't have to be long. A sentence or two about why you liked the book will do.

ABOUT THE AUTHOR

Henry Hoffman is a former newspaper editor and public library director whose works have appeared in a variety of literary and trade publications, including the Library Journal, the Midwesterner, Encyclopedia of Library Science, America: History and Life, Historical Abstracts of the United States, the Cyclopedia of Literary Places, and the Encyclopedia of Natural Disasters. He is the author of five previous novels, including Bridge to Oblivion and The Veiled Lagoon, the first two entries in the Adam Fraley mystery series. He is the recipient of the Florida Publishers Association's Gold Medal Award for Florida Fiction.

www.henryhoffman.net

ALSO BY HENRY HOFFMAN

WITH MELANGE BOOKS

Adam Fraley Mysteries

On A Midnight Clear

The Ephemeral File